# AXEL HOOLEY'S DEATH WATCH LIST

## A Sick Comedy

### Scotty-Miguel Sandoe

First Print Edition, CreateSpace September 2012
https://www.createspace.com/3750419

www.axelhooley.com
http://twitter.com/Scotty_Miguel
http://scottymiguel.com
ScottyMiguel.LA@gmail.com

Cover design by William Kent/The Kent Studios
www.thekentstudios.com

Edited by Rhonda Tinch-Mize

Author's photograph by Mark Bennington
www.benningtonheadshots.com

ISBN-10: 1478297514
ISBN-13: 978-1478297512
LCCN: 2012913617

*For Pop and Robbie,*
*who fought so bravely – and danced in the rain.*

# Contents

# Chapter 1

## The Tumble from a London Plane

It wasn't fear, but rather a sense of complete disorientation that overwhelmed him during his plunge through the branches toward the lawn. His deliberate and desperate plea for life to flash before his eyes went unanswered as he frantically grappled for an image or memory – anything that might provide a clue as to who he was or what he was or how long he had been plummeting. In the millisecond before he collided with the ground, it occurred to him to consider the possibility that he could fly. But by that time, it was too late.

It seemed idiotic to make any assessment of physical damage until he regained some sense of self. If he were a bird or a squirrel, maybe he would be alright? If he turned out to be human, on the other hand, he was completely fucked to some point obviously well beyond simple rescue.

"You okay, buddy?" The voice was distant, but near enough to trigger his sense of individuality, robbing him of the cozy feeling of oneness he had so recently shared with the Universe. Such a notion seemed ridiculous now. He could peripherally distinguish a tree and a hedge and a couple of late-model BMWs and everything else; and he was a solitary being and not part of any of it. At least he wasn't part of it any longer, if indeed he had ever been a part of anything else recently, or even historically.

He groaned and managed to roll over where his eyes met with a brown, middle-aged face that eclipsed the early morning sun. "Hey buddy? You okay?" The voice came out of the face, thickly accented and tinged with an edge of concern. The green uniform suggested that the man was some kind of landscaping or garden worker. This was comforting because it suggested a recognizable world full of homes and civilization and low-cost immigrant labor.

"Don' move, okay buddy? I get help."

He had no intention of moving, at least not in the short term. Whoever it is he might turn out to be, it was going to take some effort to fix whatever was wrong, and getting help to do it seemed like a damned good idea.

He briefly washed through various stages of semiconsciousness, but summoned enough strength to haul himself up onto his elbow and gaze down at his body – a stranger's body, naked except for a grubby pair of tighty-whities. It hurt pretty badly, but didn't appear to be missing any pieces. Of much greater concern, however, was that his form lacked all anticipated sense of familiarity. The legs were too thin for one thing, desperately pallid, and chillingly hairless. The bare feet were calloused and dirty, which might be normal enough, but the toes looked bony and vaguely skeletal. A quick check of his hands confirmed the overall frail nature of his being. The skin stretching over his arms and lanky frame was practically translucent in spots, with an overall putrefying ashen hue. If he believed in space aliens (which he certainly did not), he might have thought perhaps he was one.

At least he was making tentative contact with his beliefs. Complete self-awareness couldn't lag far behind. He didn't believe in Martians or mermaids or elves or angels and required further proof before he made any sort of commitment to the Loch Ness Monster, Bigfoot, or the giant alligators alleged to be living in the sewers beneath Manhattan.

The landscape worker trotted to keep up with the long strides of the police officer hurrying up the block toward him. They were about the same age and height, but their difference in deportment held his attention to such a degree that he failed to differentiate whether they were talking to him or about him.

"He fall from London Plane!"

The officer looked skeptically at the landscape worker who pointed upward through the thick branches of the tree. "A plane? Really? Are you sure?"

The landscape worker nodded as the police officer knelt down and placed a supportive hand under his neck. "Try not to move. An ambulance is on the way." The sunlight danced off the shiny nametag on the officer's lapel that read "Jeffries" and drew focus in an almost hypnotic fashion.

"Was I flying *to* London or *from* London?"

The officer looked at the landscape worker, who was clearly frustrated. "London Plane! London Plane!" He slapped the trunk of the tree twice, which provided emphasis but little clarity.

"Do you know how you got here?"

"I–I–I'm pretty sure I have cancer." There it was – the first absolute distinction he could recall about himself. As if being *pretty sure* instead of *absolutely certain* could somehow relocate him to a healthier setting. "That's my chemotherapy infusion unit" he said, pointing up into the tree, where a deflated bag dangled from a branch. "The blue fanny pack. Except we really shouldn't call it a *fanny pack* in case we're in England where *fanny* has a totally different meaning. I've made that mistake before, and I think the Brits are still laughing." Until he was certain he wasn't in or near London, he thought it best to censor himself.

"We're in Beverly Hills," Officer Jeffries said, somewhat proudly and as if it were obvious. "On McCarty."

At least he was home. Or close to home. Or as close to homing in on home as he was going to get, at least for now. "Beverly Hills," he sighed, smiling with relief. "Practically the Vatican."

"What?" Officer Jeffries asked, with more concern than was probably necessary.

"Practically the Vatican," he repeated, though he wasn't even sure why he said it in the first place. It felt like an echo from somewhere else, as if some antediluvian ventriloquist tapped into him from another dimension, forced the words out of his mouth, then somehow compelled him to repeat them. He was trying to rally viable clarification for Officer Jeffries as well as for himself when the same ventriloquist gave him another nudge and slammed him squarely into his identity.

His quest for self wasn't new, unfortunately – it was epic in nature and sprang from a raw and long-forgotten place just beyond memory's reach. He had always felt like, and indeed was, more of an understudy than the real McCoy. He had performed the role passably to the best of his ability for most of his 33 or 36 years (depending on your method of calculation), yet he wore himself like a secondhand suit that could never be tailored to fit. No doubt, he had never been a very good or even a particularly accurate facsimile of the precious original. He was a rushed and primitive substitute, whipstitched together from whatever scraps were handy; and no matter where this wholly inadequate stand-in fled, the elusive clues to the riddle of his own personal genesis had taken flight so long ago that they would never be found.

"My name is Axel!" he said, as if he himself were startled by the news and might require further convincing with regard to his own authenticity. "I'm Axel Hooley, and I live in Beverly Hills." As he sprawled on the ground shivering in his underpants, Axel felt obliged to attempt further explanation. "Just forget what I said about the Vatican. I don't even think I'm Catholic."

# Chapter 2

## Cedars

Zoë gave the crowded, beautifully appointed emergency room a cursory glance, then hurried on without stopping to ask questions. They had probably admitted Axel already, so she took the staff elevator to the Oncology floor. The gray pinstriped power suit she chose that morning for a settlement conference provided an intimidating shield, repellant enough that the Cedars-Sinai staff steered clear. Though she was just shy of 35, the confidence that came with her promotion to partner served her well, even when she found herself in situations completely unrelated to litigation.

Zoë had already skipped the gym and shirked a client status meeting off onto the first associate she was able to reach on her BlackBerry, which was going to go over none too well with the senior partners. Being a statuesque, well-built platinum blonde also served her well, however; she was certain she could flirt her way out of any reprimand that might come her way, and it was very likely that any such admonishment wouldn't even bother to formulate itself into an email or phone call.

Dale was tapping away on his laptop in the sixth floor lobby when Zoë got there. The haunted appearance he sported those first few months after Tommy's death had recently given way to a more alarming look of vagrancy. Dale's shaggy, brown, unkempt hair had previously been close-cropped and presumably maintained by Tommy himself, or at the very least under his watchful eye. Tommy was probably the one who picked out his clothes too for that matter, and Dale's shoddy grooming and current lack of style was a fairly accurate gauge of exactly how long Tommy had been gone. Dale's cutoffs and ratty T-shirt from some long-forgotten *Shack* concert, although certainly not inappropriate for Southern California, needed a wash, and his hair obviously hadn't been styled since the funeral. It was probably a good thing that most of his investment clients hadn't seen Dale face-to-face in years.

"What was he doing in a plane, for God's sake?" she asked. "You were supposed to be looking after him."

Dale grinned up at her – a flash of the old Dale, from before. She felt a tug deep in her chest. "He wasn't on a plane; he was in a tree."

"What was he doing in a tree, for God's sake? You were supposed to be looking after him." Zoë was pleased with herself for precisely nailing her previous tone.

"Beats the hell out of me," Dale shrugged, executing the last few keystrokes, which would no doubt purchase shares of something expensive for somebody who was probably too rich already. He closed his laptop and shook his head. "I was upstairs when they called."

"Great job, Dale. Way to go." She had only recently learned that *upstairs* was a vague euphemism for *sleeping off a hangover*. She wasn't bothered by the drinking, necessarily. If anybody had a right to alcoholism, it was probably Dale, and Axel didn't need looking after as much as he required constant rescue.

"He fell out of a tree – the name of that particular species of tree is *London Plane*. The gardener who found him didn't speak much English if you don't count the obscure names of the indigenous flora and fauna of Beverly Hills." Dale paused for effect, then continued dryly. "And oh, the laughter and merriment that surely must have ensued."

Zoë smiled in spite of herself. She didn't care if Dale was a sad sloppy drunk, his dry wit and Ivy League education never failed to shine through. "But how did he—?"

"Nobody knows. Even *he* doesn't know. I can't imagine how he got all the way to McCarty Drive on his own. I practically had to carry him up the hill on Saturday."

*The hill* was another euphemism of sorts, pertaining to Dale's home in Silverlake. There were 93 stairsteps leading from Dale's parking slab up the hill to his house. On her best day, Zoë herself could barely take the hill without an oxygen tank; and if she brought wine, she'd need a sherpa. "Your place has got to be 10 miles from Beverly Hills."

"9.2 miles, door-to-tree. I Google mapped it."

"Well, unless he's somehow mastered flight—"

"That's possible, I suppose," Dale shrugged. "Tommy's the one who never *really* got the hang of flying."

Zoë could have kicked herself for opening that particularly grim window. In the 20 odd months since Tommy's death, Dale had remained on the lookout to invoke his name at the slightest opportunity. To his credit, Dale didn't blame Axel for the death of his one and only love. Not out loud, anyway, or at least not to anybody they knew. And he easily could have, because Axel was an instigator, and Tommy was not a risk taker by nature – although accompanying Axel anyplace, even someplace as simple as a hike, always involved a certain amount of risk. And to Axel's credit, he didn't try to duck responsibility for the tragedy. Though he and Tommy were best friends, Axel had taken to referring to him as "Dale's dead boyfriend who I bullied into the open arms of the Grim Reaper."

It wasn't as if they could tiptoe forever around issues like death, or Axel's puerile approach to the world, or even the late, great Tommy Grissom. Besides, it felt like a setup, and Dale knew it was a setup, so Zoë didn't bother to apologize.

"I can take him to my place if you think that might work better." She sat next to Dale and wondered if he would let her trim those stray hairs in his ear.

"You've got the cats."

"They're *your* cats. I only took them because you've got Axel, and he's allergic."

"It's easier for me to get him to radiation," Dale said with a sense of finality. "And I think taking care of him is what Tommy would want me to do."

"Alrighty, then – as long as you're acting out of some displaced sense of responsibility, who am I to argue?"

"He'll be out of surgery in a few minutes. We can wait in his room if you want."

"Surgery?" Zoë queried with unwarranted alarm, since Dale obviously would have said something if there had been anything to say.

"His PICC line pulled out of his arm when he fell out of the tree, so they have to reinstall it, then X-ray him to be sure it's in the right place, then reconnect his chemo."

"Yuck," she said with a slight shudder. Although the mechanics of major illness were certainly no surprise, Zoë had never witnessed such workings up close. If the past two months were any indication of what was to come, the harsh treatment for Axel's illness was going to provide a broad spectrum of new and nauseating experiences for anybody who chose to stick around – and she and Dale would both be sticking.

They waited together for a few minutes in the awkward silence they sometimes found in shared moments without Axel. They were a far more likely pairing of friends than either one of them was with Axel, but Axel was the glue that held them in place.

"What was he doing in Beverly Hills?" Zoë wondered out loud.

"Maybe he was going home?" Dale speculated, though it seemed unlikely that Axel would wander so far beyond his destination, or even that he could, necessarily, given his compromised condition. The studio apartment above a garage on La Peer was still technically Axel's, but only because his landlady was so dotty and addled that she hadn't realized he'd stopped paying rent. "More to the point," Dale offered, "What was he doing in a fucking tree?"

# Chapter 3

# Shallow Roots, Widely Placed
# – Part 1

Three days after his ill-fated encounter with the thresher, the larger, arguably identifiable chunks of Axel Hooley were buried adjacent the farmhouse where Isaac and Annie Hooley hosted church services in their basement the third Sunday every other month. The Hooleys, like the larger community around them, were a devout, modest folk, preferring to deal with private matters in the traditional Amish ways. Outsiders were a necessary nuisance, of course – their livelihood largely depended on the popularity of Amish Acres, a quaint traditional village and tourist trap in nearby Nappanee, Indiana – but with regard to matters of birth and death, an entry in the flyleaf of the family Bible was generally considered more than a sufficient amount of paperwork.

Axel Hooley was different from his six older brothers in one significant respect, however – Axel had a birth certificate. Two years prior to the ill-famed thresher incident, when Isaac Hooley recognized that the urgent needs of his wife Annie were well beyond the skills of the midwife attending to Axel's birth, he wasted no time summoning outsiders for their crucial assistance, despite the somber objections of his Amish brethren. Modern hospitals and expert medical attention were necessary wonders every now and again as far as Isaac was concerned, despite the fact that such wonders often led to official recordkeeping, which in turn never came to anything of any further good to anybody.

So as far as the outside world was concerned, Axel Hooley *existed*, and if he existed, then Isaac supposed that eventually something would have to be done to make him *un*-exist. He just hoped that the circumstances of his youngest son's tragic death wouldn't be too assiduously rehashed by the outsiders, mostly for Annie's sake, as she blamed herself for allowing young Axel to toddle beyond the relative safety of the immediate barnyard.

But the days became weeks, and the weeks passed into months, which one way or another flew past two years; when eventually, as these problems sometimes do, the quandary of what was to be done about the death of Isaac and Annie's youngest boy managed to resolve itself.

The resolution to Isaac's dilemma waddled into the midst of the autumn harvest festivities and presented itself, wearing an elfin grin and a filthy diaper. Though the child was likely in search of food and comfort rather than spiritual guidance, the womenfolk readily provided the first two, then set the wheels in motion as required to supply the more divine, yet utterly essential, third element to make the toddler whole.

After some discussion among church Elders, the foundling was handed off to the still grieving Annie Hooley with the hope that a convenient and reasonable substitute might curtail her relentless weeping. Subtle inquiries were made around the village, of course, but nobody stepped up to claim the tanned child with the long dark hair.

Certainly no more than two, the toddler could scarcely pass for the late lamented youngest Hooley, who would by now have nearly reached the age of five, but Isaac imagined that wouldn't make much difference over time. As far as he was concerned, the strange child with the curious gaze had been supplied by God to relieve him of the burden of illuminating the local authorities as to the challenges, difficulties, and occasional failings that composed his simple life on the farm. Besides, a lady at the hospital had gone to all the trouble of making up a birth certificate; somebody might as well get some use out of it.

The newly anointed Axel Hooley was washed, nourished, clothed, and promptly scolded because a child of almost five years of age should no longer be in need of diapers. Annie and Isaac would keep the boy well fed and far away from the threshing machine, but New Axel was going to have to grow up some, and he was going to have to do it right quick.

Like her husband, Annie Hooley supposed that the child had been dropped from heaven in a basket. She further suspected that he was quite rightly expelled, in fact, and likely remained on several angelic watch lists specific to seraphic terrorists. Annie had raised six boys (seven if you counted Axel the first) and felt that this child's curiosity extended well beyond normal childhood inquisitiveness. It would be a miracle if New Axel managed to steer clear of the farming equipment and livestock, and if Annie or one of the boys didn't one day fling him into the thresher outright, it would be an even bigger miracle.

The Hooleys prided themselves on their benevolence, however, and took whatever challenges God provided. New Axel was cared for and tended to, and though never truly loved in the tradition of the other Hooley children, he was educated and set on a righteous path. Annie came to believe that perhaps God had very little to do with entrusting the disarming stranger into her care, but she shouldered the burden anyway and didn't complain for the most part, no matter how unusual or challenging the tiny intruder turned out to be. And oh, he was unusual and challenging beyond her wildest dreams and worst nightmares.

For one thing, New Axel never seemed to sleep, which startled Annie whenever she awoke to his otherworldly gaze. Isaac mostly steered clear of the boy, figuring that enduring the child's oddities and mischief was the price required for a good night's sleep nestled in next to a wife, no longer racked with sobs. New Axel rarely fussed, which was a blessing, but he was so unusually quiet in coming and going that Annie suspected he had somehow mastered teleportation or invisibility. New Axel could appear in an instant and vanish just as quickly with her next glance. She was never quite able to catch him in the act of vaporizing, at least not with her own eyes, though she confessed her fears to a neighbor, who had always thought Annie frivolous and a bit off-kilter to begin with. So the boy remained an outsider, despite everybody's most magnanimous efforts, and rumors always tend to follow such folk.

As the youngest child, New Axel suffered his share of poundings by the older Hooley boys, but it wasn't long before he could shinny up the nearest, tallest tree and remain there until the troubles blew over. The much older, far heavier Abner Hooley once fell and fractured his clavicle pursuing the nimble rascal up the half-dead oak that separated the Hooley land from the Fleckinger farm. New Axel was never an eager sparring partner and always obliged his pursuers to hound him to the point of collapse. He was sometimes caught, but by then his tormentor was usually too spent to inflict much damage. The Hooley Hooligans were, in many ways, the black sheep of the Amish community, and New Axel was the black sheep of the Hooleys.

The poundings came to an end around the official age of 10 when New Axel somehow convinced Amos Hooley that he was capable of harnessing the powers of the underworld and vowed to turn him into a pail of milk in his sleep. The fateful timing of ill-informed and adolescent Amos's first wet dream that night coincided so completely with the threat that the hapless boy didn't sleep well for a month.

The Amish are, historically and with rare exception, not known to be expert hustlers. This competitive void is perhaps why New Axel became such an accomplished trickster so quickly. It was a rare tourist indeed who could resist the open-faced lad in the wide-brimmed hat when approached to help secure a magazine of questionable appropriateness or sneak the eager tyke into the newest blockbuster at the Cineplex. Such straightforward forays into the *English* world were strictly forbidden, of course, but New Axel's fear of yet another trip to the woodshed was greatly outmatched by his insatiable curiosity. Besides, it was clear that he wasn't going to learn much more about the world from the Hooleys. They and their brethren had, after all, attempted to stop all forward movement of any kind a hundred or so odd years ago.

The Hooleys encouraged reading and personal growth, assuming that such activities were inspired by and limited to the Holy Bible, which New Axel read cover to cover under duress. While some of the tales were interesting, and he liked the bit with the whale, he found the material to be a labor-intensive and tedious read. And he had long since decided he wanted no part of the angry, vengeful Old Testament God everybody kept threatening him with. The worst beatings of his life were administered in the name of righteousness. He couldn't help but think that wherever He was, God probably had bigger fish to fry, and if He didn't want New Axel to occasionally sneak a peek at a titty magazine, He probably shouldn't have invented titties in the first place. And making him so darn curious about them merely in order to have him flogged in His holy name just seemed mean-spirited and not in keeping with what he hoped was the gentler nature of a universe chock full of titties.

The Good Book offered some interesting stories and solid rules to live by – don't kill people, be nice to your parents, and the like. New Axel eventually reckoned the Bible mostly continued to exist in the modern world in order to prevent the stupid people from fucking the animals.

Not surprisingly, dawning sexual awareness descended on the teen, or rather, preteen New Axel, like a Hoosier tornado. The apple-cheeked Amish girls, kept at a distance by tradition and the dozens of watchful eyes of the Brethren, were wooed in clandestine assignations. Rumors of sexual experimentation soon flooded the barn raisings and sewing circles. By Amish standards, New Axel was absolutely exotic – dark featured and impishly small for his legal and official age. That, coupled with his inherent lack of respect for tradition and authority, drew the eager and repressed young lasses like hogs to the trough.

While New Axel's seductive skills would have been rudimentary and laughable under ordinary circumstances, they worked their magic remarkably well in Amish Acres. He had, after all, the experience of several years of cinema attendance working for him, along with a growing collection of pornography squirreled away in the grain silo. So as fears for the vestal virgins of Amish Acres grew, the Elders resolved that something must be done quickly about the outsider they'd taken in but never truly embraced. The possibility that the young interloper might soon leave a permanent reminder of his injection into their community and their womenfolk was a growing concern.

Thus, on the day the problematic birth certificate proclaimed Axel Hooley to be 16 years of age – the agreed-upon yardstick for Amish adulthood – New Axel was abruptly thrust into the *English* world as a result of traditional and fortuitous *Rumspringa.*

*Rumspringa* literally translates to "running around" – the unofficial period for Amish youth between childhood and the hopeful decision to choose baptism into the Amish church. In some Amish communities, boys experiment by dressing *English*, driving, drinking, or living on their own for a time: the commonly held attitude being that the outside world should be experienced, then rejected in favor of a simple life closer to God. The girls generally experimented less, but a certain amount of carousing was conveniently ignored. Rumspringa is commonly tolerated rather than encouraged, but in New Axel's case, it became an absolute requirement.

Isaac and Annie took New Axel for a long walk the night before his departure to provide what little information they could of his origins, or at least to recap the most often repeated rumors. While the boy's true parents may have merely been vagabonds, Isaac thought it likely they had enough of a working knowledge of the community to ascertain the most suitable time and place for successful child abandonment. A small circus had set down nearby for a few days that summer, and the actors who descended on the Round Barn Theatre every spring for the annual production of *Plain & Fancy* always seemed an oversexed and irresponsible bunch, so both were put forth as options should New Axel wish to ponder his true heritage further. But the real truth was that nobody had an inkling where New Axel had come from, nobody had done any real investigating, and whatever clues may have once existed had long since disappeared.

Annie was certain that New Axel's mother and father had not been married, by whatever reasoning Annie used to draw her simple conclusions, and broke the tragic news to New Axel that he was almost certainly a bastard. New Axel wouldn't have minded so much, but Annie was deeply troubled by this reasonable certainty and assured him that such a sinful burden would be a difficult one that must be borne well into eternity. According to *Deuteronomy 23:2, "A bastard shall not enter into the congregation of the Lord, even to his tenth generation shall he not enter into the congregation of the Lord."* Annie took this to mean that, even had New Axel been a pious and decent soul, he would never gain entry to the Kingdom of Heaven, nor would the 10 generations that may follow. New Axel was only troubled to the extent that he had been threatened, beaten and coerced into reading the friggin' Gospel night after night in what was apparently a senseless and mean-spirited exercise. New Axel hoped that at least this revelation would take the pressure off from here on out – or at least until the day he was to be damned forever to writhe in the fiery pits of Hell under the glowing red watchful eyes of Satan.

Unwilling to be further buggy whipped as he was unceremoniously booted out the door, New Axel pointed out to Isaac and Annie the Good Book's prior passage, *Deuteronomy 23:1: "He that is wounded in the stones, or hath his privy member cut off, shall not enter into the congregation of the Lord."* When it became clear they weren't following his logic, New Axel suggested that, depending on the specifics of what the thresher had or had not done to the *stones* or *privy member* of Old Axel lo and behold those many years ago, they might not find *his* little pink cherub plucking away on a harp up in heaven, either. Annie nearly fainted, and she didn't share further words with New Axel until she said goodbye at the bus station.

So, with his birth certificate tucked into a worn-but-still-good valise, New Axel was presented with a bus ticket out of town and 140 dollars collected from nearly every father with a daughter of courting age in the county. Annie Hooley gave the boy a sincere kiss goodbye, and shared with Isaac the community's collective sigh of relief as they watched him go.

While he knew he was never coming back and would be shunned henceforward, and even though he had some sense of the reasons why, New Axel was quite moved to see dozens of the brethren accompany him to the bus station for his send-off. He had taken two catnaps on the bus before it dawned on him that the well-wishers were probably present only to ensure his bona fide departure.

New Axel was young and strong. He could raise a barn, castrate a hog, and plow a right smart piece of land with remarkable speed. With all that going for him, he knew that he wouldn't starve. Of greater worry was the nagging feeling that he had forgotten something important. It was as if he had left something behind, yet couldn't put his finger on what, exactly, it could be. Whatever it was, it had been left so far behind that it was well beyond reach, because he was certain he hadn't left anything important back at Amish Acres.

New Axel decided that his years with the Amish brethren weren't altogether bad if you didn't count what turned out to be all that futile emphasis on the Scripture, but now he was off to see what lay beyond. The singular Axel Hooley left on earth, the un-holiest of the Hooley Hooligans, the bad boy of Amish Acres, was about to find out what surprises the world held.

# Chapter 4

# The Maple Leafs

"C'mon, *please!* It's just eight dollars. That's like a 25 percent discount or something." Axel whined like a child, but that was just part of their game. Dale looked at the bright blue foam maple leaf encircling Axel's puffy bald face – it *did* go nicely with the light blue surgical mask that was intended to filter out the assorted Staples Center germs before they booked passage into his lungs.

Hockey was not one of the larger draws for the sizeable arena, particularly on a weeknight when most Angelinos had already fought traffic twice, so Axel assumed that the inner city youth working the tchotchkes kiosk had nothing better to do than barter with him.

"If I told you how much I'm spending on your treatment, you wouldn't even have the nerve to ask me for food," Dale assured him.

"If I don't die, I'll reimburse you. Just keep a running total."

"You'd have to give back to back hand jobs for 200 years to make that kind of money."

"Eight bucks will buy you more laughs than whatever it is you're spending to poison me with chemo and turn me radioactive." Axel paused, not entirely certain that was true.

"Besides, Toronto is *your* team, ya fuckin' Canuck. I'm only trying to be supportive. I don't even know if I *like* hockey."

"If you really want to be supportive, you'll catch your breath so we can go find our seats." A rational person would have told Axel to shut up long before now, but Dale was too well-bred for his own good. A native of Vancouver, Dale was indeed more of a Canuck fan than the Toronto Maple Leafs, but hockey was hockey, and everything in the tiny northern province of Canada seemed to bleed together in the arbitrary storybook land of Axel.

Axel took several deliberate deep breaths and stood up. Even with VIP parking, he needed to stop and rest twice on the way into the arena. He looked like shit, and he felt like even shoddier shit, but he had talked his way out of the house, and he wasn't about to give up on the head gear. Dale could see him preparing to launch a final pitch, so he supplied a preemptive and uncharacteristically firm, "No."

Axel clutched at the boy's sleeve, and his eyelids dropped to half-mast. "Please, kind sir – I'm dying of cancer – may I keep the hat?" The young proprietor nodded apprehensively, as if denying a deathbed request might trigger cataclysmic karmic repercussions. Axel's eyes flooded with crocodile tears as he threw his arms around the horrified youth and muttered "Bless you. God bless you and your immortal soul," with what sounded like his dying breath. Dale pulled Axel off the kid and led him away before he could inflict further trauma.

When they were out of earshot, Axel slapped his way out of Dale's grasp. "I can't believe you made me play the cancer card, you prick."

"I wish you would stop doing that. You're not going to die," Dale sighed.

"Statistically speaking, death has a 100 percent rate of success, at least with regard to carbon-based life forms, but you're right – I'll probably be the exception."

Dale didn't bother reiterating that Axel wasn't going to die *now* or *of stomach cancer*. Pursuing it would only result in Axel building a case for his own imminent demise. And Dale supposed that it could happen, though such an outcome would more likely result from the treatment than from the disease itself.

Axel's initial diagnosis came about by accident, resulting from the physical exam and blood test required for a part-time job at a Beverly Hills gym and day spa. The pending job offer was quickly withdrawn, presumably based on the grim diagnosis.

The diagnosis was Stage 2 (T1) stomach cancer, which meant that the cancer had only reached the lining of the stomach, but nine nearby lymph nodes also contained cancer cells. So cancer had already packed up its evil offspring and sent them off to college. This was bad news, but certainly not horrible news in the age of radiation and chemotherapy and hope, as portrayed in *Lifetime* movies by nobodies (who usually survived) and in cinematic releases by Meryl Streep or Debra Winger (who usually didn't). The horrible news was not having adequate medical insurance, and if Axel didn't make it, there would be no cheery consequences for those who stuck by him. At least Shirley MacLaine had won a Best Actress Oscar for her support.

Worse news came a few weeks later when it was determined that Axel had a *"dihydropyrimidine dehydrogenase"* deficiency, which in simple terms meant that he was missing the necessary enzyme that would assist his body's elimination processes to cleanse the chemotherapy out of his system – the "DPD" enzyme. It was a disorder rare enough that there wasn't even a test for it. If chemotherapy was accompanied by alarmingly high fevers, hallucinations, severe nausea, or uncommon combinations of side effects, some kind of DPD deficiency was possibly present; and in Axel's case, was all but certain.

When asked about his family medical history, Axel explained to his Oncologist that he had been raised by jackals and the only information he could provide was that there was no information to be had.

Dale and Zoë were the only two friends Axel had told of his illness, at least as far as Dale knew. The news was troublesome and inconvenient, and Axel didn't have the social finesse to spread the word without traumatizing the hordes. Dale and Zoë stumbling into the chaos was unavoidable, as Axel's free associating mental riffs inevitably spewed forth enough clues to complete the puzzle.

Following his first round of fluorouracil chemotherapy – otherwise known as 5FU – Axel became neutropenic, which meant that his white blood cells (specifically his *neutrophil granulocytes*) dropped so dangerously low that he was threatened by bacterial infections and neutropenic sepsis: symptoms of which included fevers and tremors. Fortunately, his doctors reacted quickly with hydration and antibiotics. He also had to avoid fresh fruits and vegetables, plants, crowds, the outdoors, and anything having had a recent or cozy relationship with dirt. With round one of chemotherapy complete, radiation was suspended for two weeks to allow his body to regroup and his white cells to rally for round two, which ultimately led to his perplexing nocturnal journey into Beverly Hills.

Though feeble and exhausted, Axel had begged to venture out when he discovered that a client had sent Dale the hockey tickets. And Dale had relented when Axel Googled *"O, Canada"* so that he could sing along at the appropriate moment because resisting at that point would have been futile. Axel hadn't done badly with the lyrics, though he substituted *"We stand on guard for thee"* with *"We stand on cars and freeze."* Dale appreciated the effort nonetheless and overlooked the new lyric because it still worked.

Dale couldn't enjoy the match because keeping an eye on Axel took both eyes and most of his focus. As with all public events, Axel was captivated by the crowd, the vendors, the jumbotrons, the gum stuck to the bottom of his seat by previous patrons, the bright chaser lights, and anything vaguely shiny. Chemotherapy had dulled his rapidly idling senses, which surprisingly didn't help even one little bit with regard to his limited attention span.

The Maple Leafs led the Kings by a significant margin, so Dale thought it best to remove Axel from the crowd at the beginning of the third period, which Axel had already managed to refer to as the *final quarter*, the *ninth inning*, and the *tenth frame*. Dale was unalarmed because even if Axel had been in his right mind, the subtle differences in rules and time periods between any two sporting events would still have been a lost cause.

They were resting on a bench outside the stadium when an over-the-hill hipster on a cell phone whipped out a cigarette and asked, "Do one of you have a light?" Dale cringed and braced himself because whatever was coming couldn't possibly be good.

"I have cancer, asshole." Axel hoisted himself to his feet and headed toward the car without waiting for a response. Dale envied Axel's freedom, though he didn't always appreciate being in his orbit. Axel's brain usually engaged sometime well after his mouth was off and running, and he was lucky that his overall spirited nature and intimidating height generally protected him from trouble. Dale supposed that Axel was now shielded by whatever supernatural forces were in place to protect drunks, imbeciles, and the hopelessly infirm.

"Do you want to drive?" It wasn't the wisest offer Dale had ever proffered, but he knew that Axel was having difficulty letting go of the freedoms that come with fitness. He thought getting him behind the wheel again might help.

"You're not serious?" The Lexus was relatively new and top-of-the-line, and Dale was not widely known for throwing caution to the wind. "You only had a few beers, right?" In truth, Axel hadn't monitored Dale's beer intake and had no idea what to expect.

Dale chucked Axel the keys, which bounced off his jacket and dropped to the ground. "You're still a better bet in case there are alcohol checkpoints."

"Holy fuck, Dale, my eyesight's mad blurry from the chemo. You really don't care what happens to you, do you?"

Axel picked up the keys, unlocked the car, and they got in. He rested as he adjusted the luxurious driver's pod and mirrors to fit his gangly frame. Before he started the car, he turned solemnly to Dale. "Do you think that maybe I'm black?" Dale didn't respond. "Not totally black, of course. But maybe a little?"

Dale could tell the question was sincere, so he didn't laugh. He gave Axel's familiar features a once-over. They were both technically around 36, though Axel's true age was thought to be somewhat younger. He'd looked younger too, until recently, but now he was looking worn and haggard and old. Axel could possibly be Greek or Italian or Latin or Jewish or Middle Eastern, or any number of mystifying combinations, but Dale saw no obvious outward signs of African ancestry. "Maybe. Why do you ask?"

"My Oncologist said that DPD deficiency is more common in blacks than whites."

"That doesn't mean you're black, Axel. It doesn't really mean anything, necessarily."

Axel hadn't really expected confirmation from Dale and would have laughed if he'd gotten it. Dale couldn't be expected to understand – his family's lineage was well documented on both sides. He had a coat of arms hanging in his living room, for God's sake. "I know. It's like I'm composed of these useless tidbits, and sort of vaguely identifying one of them doesn't change anything. I probably need to stop thinking that it will."

Axel gingerly put the car in gear and carefully headed out of the parking structure. "I jus' hope the bruthus don' catch me wheelin' 'roun this middle-age cracka-box. I needs me some *rims* or somethin', I gonna be drivin' yo hack."

The drive to Silverlake was uncharacteristically steady and more meticulous and careful than anything Dale had ever witnessed Axel do up to that point, as if he were rallying his remaining clarity to compensate for the hack job the drugs were doing on him. After successfully negotiating his way onto Dale's parking slab, Axel took a brief time-out before trekking up to the house. If he had saved any of his get-up-and-go for the hike up the hill, it certainly wasn't evident to Dale, who had to drag him most of the way. Dale didn't complain, though he worried that Axel might reach the point where he would no longer be able to make the journey with minor assistance and might have to be carried.

The attention Axel currently demanded allowed Dale to put off dealing with his own issues, and that was exactly the way he wanted it. Axel fading away slowly in his downstairs den kept Dale connected to Tommy in a peculiar way that couldn't possibly be healthy, but again, he didn't care. If that was the only connection he could make, he would take it. And if he could save Axel, it might in some small way help him get past losing Tommy. Maybe it wouldn't; but Axel urgently needed saving, and he and Zoë had emerged as the most likely candidates to do it.

Axel had taken up residence in the downstairs den in order to chase Dale back upstairs to the big, empty California King he had shared with Tommy. Besides, the den had cable and a fast wireless connection, and the furniture was overstuffed and warm and cozy. Dale had spent the months since Tommy's death sleeping downstairs, and Axel figured that if there was healing to be done, the downstairs den had been established as the place to do it.

After the incident in Beverly Hills, Axel had consented to being handcuffed to the sofa at night for his own protection. Dale held the key, however, and was a notoriously heavy sleeper. Unable to access the bathroom the first night, Axel dragged the sofa part of the way into the hall so that he could take a dump into a potted palm that died two days later from exposure to whatever mixture of chemicals were sent to assassinate his abnormal cells, so obviously new arrangements were going to be required.

Axel decided that if he were going to die in a fire or earthquake, in what investigators would no doubt determine to be a compromising position, he might as well throw in the towel and let the cancer get him. Not that the notion of a little scandal there at the end had lost its appeal entirely, of course.

So now he was handcuffed to the elegant neck of a wooden art deco greyhound dog. Axel couldn't tell if the greyhound was tacky, or just some kind of sophisticated good taste that he failed to understand. Dale had assured him that, even if it were made of the more traditional marble, it would be tacky. The greyhound in question was fashioned of mahogany and in such unforgivably poor taste that it could only have been a housewarming gift from Dale's housekeeper who breezed in on Thursdays to sweep up for the weekend. The greyhound had some heft, but was mobile enough to drag around efficiently, and would theoretically permit bathroom access and possible escape from natural disaster; though wearing handcuffs would still require more explaining than he would ever be able to comfortably manage.

Axel resisted giving his petrified pet a name because he did not wish their association to be ongoing and thought it best not to form any sort of attachment beyond what was absolutely necessary.

As he drifted off to sleep, Axel reckoned that if he had possessed any shred of his former self, he would have asked Dale what he was doing with a set of handcuffs. It was always the quiet ones with the uptown manners that harbored the coolest and most unlikely secrets. At least that's what Axel hoped, for Dale's sake.

# Chapter 5

# The Twiggs

Beulah and Carver Twigg were widely regarded as the most hateful, mean-spirited couple in all of Rutherford County. There was talk, in fact, that their unsavory reputation had reached well beyond Murfreesboro, all the way into Nashville.

The locals who frequented Beulah's Roadside Diner – in Smyrna just east of the 24 – did so mostly out of habit or lack of geographically viable options. Besides, Beulah pretty much stayed in the kitchen when she could, and Carver was up at the house most days, lost in a ratty plaid couch littered with beer cans and turkey jerky wrappers. Even when he did drag himself down to the Diner, he usually just sat on the porch, whittled, and scowled out at the road.

Not that Carver couldn't turn on the charm when he needed to, or that he didn't pull his weight. Every now and again, the help would up and run off – tired of the abuse most likely, and the promise of a payday that never came. So whenever the crucial circumstance arose, Carver put on a clean shirt, stuck his teeth into his mouth, and drove to the bus station in Nashville, where he'd pluck a fresh-faced new runaway to work the Diner. Carver was of a mind that curvaceous young ladies made the best kinda help, but there had been a fuss a while back, and now

Beulah insisted on having a boy to wait the tables and wash up the dishes. And Carver knew better than to cross a vindictive whore-cunt like Beulah, so that's how they ended up with the sweet natured Amish kid.

Now Beulah was happy because she had her a boy, and the tips she confiscated from him at the end of each day were bigger because the regulars seemed to have taken a shine to him. And Carver was happy because the boy was accustomed to hard work and didn't mind mowin' the yard and clearin' stumps on what had traditionally been the help's day off. The boy had asked for his pay a couple of times, but he hadn't flapped around much when Carver put him off yet another week. It had been a month already, and Carver figured the boy for a fool and hoped to get another few weeks of free work out of him before he up and disappeared.

The boy, on the other hand, had already been plotting his escape; it just didn't play out in any of the ways he or the Twiggs had anticipated.

Tuesday mornings were usually slow and the only customers left by 10:30 were an older hippie couple, who were making their way across the country in a beat-up Jeep Cherokee. They were friendly and chatty, and Axel didn't see any point in disappointing them when they invited him to pull up a chair. It didn't take much prodding for Axel's entire story, brief as it was, to come pouring out while he wolfed down a big plate of the fried mess Beulah thrust through the service window at him. The old hippies seemed interested in his journey from northern Indiana all the way to his current situation sleeping on a makeshift bed of milk crates in the storage room.

But Beulah smelled trouble brewing before long, so she shoved her pale sweaty face far enough out of the kitchen to be heard. "You still got them breakfast dishes, boy!"

"Right now ah'm eatin' me some 'taters and jawin' with these nice folks, so them dishes can hold their dang horses." It had only taken a few weeks for Axel's quaint, vaguely Norwegian-sounding Amish accent to give way to the harsh drawl of the northern Tennessee locals. That was all Beulah needed to hear,

26

and she was out the back door like a shot, puffing her way up toward the house. If Carver was good for anything, it was putting the fear of God into the help. She didn't want to lose the boy – he was a tidy combination of speedy robust politeness most days and kept up with his chores, but she would not have him sassin' back. If that meant Carver had to pay him a little bit every now and again or beat him with a plank, so be it; but Beulah would not tolerate a smart mouth.

Carver could tell them hippies was up to no good as soon as he saw 'em all hunched over, plotting with the boy. Probably out to steal somebody else's help without messing with the necessary legwork or grueling training program. "Boy, I need to see you in the goddamn kitchen *now!*"

Carver was already dressed and on his way out for some poker when Beulah intercepted him in the driveway. The recent boost in tips was making Beulah soft, so she hadn't noticed Carver skimming the bank deposits to fund his hobby, and a recent run of good luck had parlayed a few hundred bucks into nearly a thousand, and today all of 'em was burning a hole in his pocket. He was determined to finish with the boy and get to the game, and he was further infuriated when the boy loped into the kitchen without a goddamn care in the world. Carver smacked him hard across the face, causing the boy to stumble to catch his balance. He wasn't hurt bad. Hell, the boy was fast, in good shape, and could probably give the older man a run for his money if he took it into his head to turn mean. But Carver knew mean, and he knew stupid, and he saw a heap of the latter in the boy and diddly-squat of the former.

The boy shook his head and steadied himself, then ducked into the storage room only to return a split second later with his ratty-assed suitcase. "If you'll just pay me my wages, Mr. Twigg, I'll be on my way."

"I ain't payin' you nothin', boy. Not 'til you finish washin' them dishes like you was told." No sense admitting that the boy was never gonna see a dime.

The boy cocked his head like a spaniel trying to interpret a complex series of training cues. Carver nodded toward the dishes soaking in the sink. The boy shook his head slowly and moved toward the door. "I'll just be on my way, then."

But Carver blocked his way, puffing himself up to his full height, which he imagined could be pretty intimidating. He showed no fear, despite the boy's superior speed and reflexes. "You ain't goin' nowhere, boy. Gimme that suitcase and get them motherfuckin' dishes washed."

Carver flicked his blade open and cut a swath of air in front of him with slow, expert slices. He was called *Carver* for a reason, after all. And if this dumb Amish boy thought he was going to make a fool out of Carver Twigg, he had another think a comin'. Them hippies'd think twice about snatchin' a boy with a couple jagged scars across his pretty face.

Axel slowly pulled a skillet out of the sink and hefted it in a manner that was more curious than threatening as he backed toward the stove. It felt heavy and could probably do some damage, he thought, though matters of weight, density, and velocity were largely uncharted and mysterious waters. Still, a hurtling skillet might buy him a little time to reach the door with his tattered valise and his precious birth certificate.

Axel was peaceful by nature and completely unaware of his own blossoming strength – and Carver saw that peaceful nature backed up by what looked to be a strict Amish upbringing, so he reckoned that he had the upper hand. Axel squeezed his eyes closed and threw hard and wide, missing Carver by a country mile.

Carver grinned a gummy smile as the skillet landed behind him with a dull thud. The boy's hand flew to his mouth in terror as Carver advanced. It wasn't until he heard the low moan from behind him that Carver turned to see blood spurting from Beulah's ruined nose as she dropped to her knees and then flopped onto her face. Dumb bitch couldn't even walk into a room without finding trouble.

On her best day, Beulah had never been a beauty, not by a longshot, not even in her youth, but Carver tolerated her so long as she faced the wall while he was taking his manly pleasure and didn't talk none or distract him with needless moaning. But

Carver was going to have one hell of a time conjuring up any fantasy material with Beulah's blood-spurtin' face haunting him.

That's when Carver Twigg knew he was gonna kill the boy. He'd slice him up right here in the kitchen and bury the body out in the field. The kid was a drifter, so nobody was gonna come around asking after him. He'd already been through the boy's things and knew he didn't have anything of value. These are the thoughts that passed through Carver's mind in the moment before he was taken out by the second hurtling iron skillet of the day – the hot one from the stove that still had charred bacon smoldering in it.

Axel no longer had the patience for the particulars of the Diner's payroll procedures, but he figured his coffee can full of tips and the cash he lifted from Carver's wallet before he bolted out the door would have to do. It wasn't until later that he realized he hadn't done too badly for his first few weeks on his own.

Beulah's regular customers were no help at all by the time the sheriff got around to questioning them about the robbery. Most couldn't even recall a boy working at the Diner, let alone a mischievous Amish boy. Those that had any recollection whatsoever were, like Carver and Beulah, completely unable to remember the boy's name. Descriptions of the accused varied widely – authorities were directed to look for, in turn – a hunchback of Hispanic descent, a pre-op transsexual, a young black man who resembled one of the lesser-known Harlem Globetrotters, and a fat, balding albino. A woman of 93 who ate breakfast at Beulah's every morning, recalled that the boy resembled Norma Desmond or Omar Sharif; but in either case, they should most definitely be on the lookout for someone in a turban.

Beaulah and Carver soon came to hate their regulars even more than they despised that goddamn Amish boy.

# Chapter 6

# A Breeze Through the Boughs

The strong Santa Ana winds hadn't technically woken Axel up. Not really, anyway; they had merely facilitated the awareness that he wasn't asleep. This was a new pattern – he no longer awakened, but rather drifted into the dawning realization that he was no longer sleeping, if indeed he had even slept at all. He supposed that under the circumstances, any temporary lack of self-awareness was a relief.

It was 3:17 in the morning according to the cable television box. Axel tucked his mahogany greyhound under his arm and padded down the hall toward the bathroom. Zoë was having another sleepover on the living room sofa, a habit she'd fallen into in recent weeks. She worried that Axel might become too substantial a burden for Dale, so she hired a cat sitter for the two cats that weren't even hers and showed up with takeout almost every night. Dale didn't wish to inconvenience Zoë, so he often prepared dinner in anticipation of her arrival in a futile effort to make her stop pushing the junk food. Thus the two stood vigil and at a standoff most evenings, listening to Axel's muddled, repetitive conversation and observations – another side effect of the chemotherapy – and sharing worried glances. Three times that evening, he had commented that one of them should have become an Oncologist because they were obviously desperate to find ways to help.

Axel's sense of taste had fled, and he was usually too nauseous to eat anyway, so he felt like even more of an ingrate for rejecting the massive amounts of food provided. He watched them pick their way through both meals during the long evenings and worried that if the cycle proceeded to one of its more obvious conclusions, he would eventually be mourned by a pair of overachieving thirtysomething fat people.

Axel paused to listen to the peaceful cadence of Zoë's breathing in contrast to the strong breezes outside. How long would they have the patience for him? He was exhausting the two people he could least afford to wear out, and he felt powerless to alter his circumstances.

Zoë had printed out an article for him from the New York Times explaining "Chemo Brain" – a proven phenomena in which chemotherapy so scrambles the thought processes that personality becomes largely submerged. That was the gist of it anyway. Axel didn't understand the article completely, probably because he had a nasty case of chemo-brain. The article did confirm what Axel already suspected – his essence was ebbing away, bit by bit.

He and his gentle mentor, Rachel, had long ago engaged in lengthy discussions about the soul and what it was or wasn't and the kind of potential with which it may have gifted mankind. As usual, she had perhaps left him too much room for his own thoughts and interpretations. If his soul wandered off, what sense was there in reviving its carrying case? He usually prevented himself from thinking about such things, but he no longer had the authority to keep his mind from wandering.

Axel hadn't thought about Rachel in a long time, and merely calling her forth as some kind of teacher didn't do her justice. She was about the best stand-in for a mother he would ever know, but even that portrayal didn't honor her the way Axel would have liked it to. If he thought about Rachel and Tad too much, he would probably cry, and he wasn't going to give in to that kind of self-pity. Not yet, or at least not right now. Still . . .

what would he give for ten minutes of undivided attention from his sorely missed *de facto* parents? Not even ten – five minutes would do. He was just that desperate.

Axel remembered that he was going to the bathroom, decided that he didn't really need to pee, and returned to the den, banging the onerous greyhound on the archway as he rounded the corner. He opened up his laptop and logged on.

This whole fiasco felt like a major thesis defense for which he hadn't adequately prepared. He needed to make a better plan. He wanted to survive without killing Dale and Zoë off with exhaustion and worry, and he needed to launch such a plan before his next round of chemo when things might get worse.

His friends were good ones, but he had never thought to test them to find out exactly how good. Like his DPD deficiency, he supposed, some situations are so rare and unusual that there just isn't a test for them. His motley group of comrades were rare and unusual too, so with some luck maybe some of them would make the grade.

Axel had deliberately kept most everyone in the dark about his illness in order to spare them any anxiety and to save himself the burden of delivering such grim news. There wasn't much overlap among his crowd as they were mostly strangers to one another, and they were going to be none too happy about being misled, that was for sure. He emitted a long exhale intended to discharge the last of his pride and began typing.

> Greetings, Everyone:
>
> I have cancer. Stomach cancer to be specific, and it's reached my lymph system. Sorry to be so abrupt, but there it is – now you know why I've been avoiding you. I don't understand everything that's happening, but I probably need to do as I'm told and take care of myself if I want to get through this.
>
> I'm staying at Dale Oakley's homo-den-of-iniquity in Silverlake right now, but I hope to return to my apartment in BH, assuming that

things resolve sooner rather than later. Dale is taking great care of me, along with loyal friend Zoë Beecher; but I'd like them to stop hovering and get on with their regular lives to whatever degree possible, which is why I hope you might be able to pitch in if necessary.

I have no family except for those of you reading this – I think most of you know that already. So now I find myself in a place where I have to ask for your help. Please know this is not an obligation – you have my absolute love and adoration no matter how this plays out.

To be honest, I'm not even sure what it is I'm asking of you. A ride to my daily radiation appointments? An emergency refill on my anti-nausea meds? Maybe just a sympathetic ear to bitch into for an hour or so? I just don't know. Right now I'd like somebody to remind me that I'm strong and funny and (if not actually brainy) perhaps occasionally insightful, as I seem to have lost my grip on all of that.

If I am compelled to issue some sort of SOS in the weeks to come, please let me know if I am welcome to reach out to you.

Yours,

Axel

P.S.: A contact sheet is attached so that you can reach each other. If anybody wants to opt out, I apologize for dispersing your personal infor-mation with such wild abandon.

Axel found drafting the email to be both humbling and cathartic, then questioned the necessity of actually sending it. His whole body hurt, but he couldn't tell if it was physical or emotional in origin, and decided it was probably both. He eyed the bottle of OxyContin on the bookshelf. Dr. Kenn had examined him after the incident on McCarty drive and jumped him right into the powerful Schedule II family of drugs. Dale Googled "OxyContin" when they got home, and one of the first hits was an article entitled *Hillbilly Heroin*.

Axel had thus far resisted the urge to indulge in whatever relief the enchanted pills might provide, worried that they might rob him of his experiences. The treatment for cancer was probably vicious and horrible and challenging for a very good reason – the human body could only endure so much ravaging, after all, before dying began to look like a damned attractive option. Wasn't he supposed to go through this and maybe learn something? The perceived wisdom of cancer survivors was probably overrated, but he wasn't sure that he wanted to take that chance. Axel hadn't reached a point where his fear of survival outweighed his fear of death, but he was afraid that day might come, and that's probably what the OxyContin was there for. The two aspirin he took earlier were useless. Dale had called the aspirin *Amish Analgesics*, which Axel forgot to laugh at until now.

Upon discovering that Axel had no known relatives, Dr. Kenn sat with him and spoke quietly. "You might be surprised at the people who step forward and come through for you now." But before Axel could revel in the encouragement, the good doctor countered with a grim warning: "You may also be surprised at those who don't."

Fuck it, the dreaded email was the only solution he could come up with. Axel had to send it, and he needed to figure out to whom he was going to hurl the electronic bombshell. To begin with, they had to be local. Friends scattered hither and yon weren't much use in an emergency. Axel racked his brain to shake loose the folks who wouldn't necessarily go ballistic or fall apart at receiving a call in the middle of the night.

Axel thought hard about the most stalwart and trustworthy of the riffraff that composed his left-coast clique and pictured the candidates dutifully stepping in line to form a tiny battalion:

*Maude Jarvis* – Maude had been an associate professor under Rachel back in the day. She currently taught religious studies part-time at UCLA and might be helpful if his soul required grease in order to return to home plate or move onward. She had been in a severe auto accident during her move to Los Angeles that required months of recovery, and still walked with a pronounced limp. Maude understood suffering, knew when to fight, and knew when to surrender.

*Rhymey Lambright* – A refugee from an Amish community in Pennsylvania, Rhymey was introduced to Axel by one of his massage therapy clients. Rhymey had fled the simple life in favor of a comparatively glamorous career as a Hollywood screen extra. Rhymey's "life as the atmosphere" as he called it, was limited because he was afraid to drive and never ever took freeways. But Rhymey was a great guy, and if you could disregard the freeway issue, probably one of the most self-sufficient souls in Los Angeles County or anywhere else. Besides, you never knew when you might need help harnessing an ox.

*Tyrell Martin* – The former drug dealer worked mostly as a counselor to inner-city youth, though he wasn't officially affiliated with any formal organization. His altruistic efforts could be funded with actual drug money for all Axel knew. Tyrell was teaching Axel to play basketball, and in exchange Axel promised to teach Tyrell how to snow ski. If Tyrell showed as much skill on the slopes as Axel showed on the basketball court, the hilarity that was in store might be worth recovering for. Tyrell was a great guy and seemed to know how to get impossible things done.

*Cheryl and Claude Vogel* – The Vogels were from the upper peninsula of Michigan – "Yoopers" – who owned a microbrewery prior to retiring to the San Fernando Valley so that Cheryl could stalk David Duchovny. They worked part-time at a medical marijuana clinic in West Hollywood and had a contraption in their garage that distilled a health drink that was practically moonshine. They were good-hearted, generous Midwestern folks, jolly and content most all the time. Their potential contribution to Axel's comfort and well-being was so obvious he couldn't believe he hadn't thought of it until now.

*Partho Mishra* – Partho was only twelve or so when he fell into Axel's circle at a coffeehouse where he made a pest of himself until Axel bought him a latte. Partho's father was an envoy of the Indian film industry – the public face of Bollywood in Hollywood. Axel and Partho often went biking or hiking on weekends. His 16th birthday had just passed, and he would certainly have a driver's license and a nice car by now. Partho also apparently had no proper adult supervision; otherwise, why was he allowed to spend weekends in remote mountain areas with a former stripper? Then Axel remembered that Partho's mother had died of cancer when he was just a young child, so he promptly struck him from the list. Partho was young, after all. Then again . . . like Axel, Partho's life had been comprised of major events he was unprepared for, and he had done alright. Axel decided that including him would be okay.

*Sylvia Belzer* – Sylvia lived in Beverly Hills six months before God laid the bedrock and was already middle-aged when she bedded both Dean Martin and one of the Monkees on the same weekend. She'd been married four times – three of which were lucrative, two of which were love, and one that was just a mistake gotten out of the way early. She knew everybody, loved everybody, fondly remembered the old days at Chasen's, and still enjoyed dinner at the Dresden Room or a cabaret singer at the Roosevelt as long as she got her nap in the afternoon. Axel had installed and removed three sets of mysteriously unsatisfactory kitchen cabinets in Sylvia's home before he understood that she was just fond of having people around and liked to chat. Yes, she was getting up there in years, but nothing could shake Sylvia Belzer. Not a single goddamn thing.

*Esperanza Baum* – Esperanza's history was even more exotic than Axel's own. An illegal alien, Esperanza briefly worked as a maid for Sylvia, who introduced the then 19-year old to her octogenarian brother Adam. Esperanza immediately married him for citizenship before realizing he was in it for real. The fiery

Latina was a good sport about it apparently, because whatever pleasures she provided on their wedding night killed the dear little man six days later. According to Sylvia, he went out with a bang ("the good kind"). Esperanza's charge cards still read "Mrs. Adam Baum," which really must have cracked up the girls behind the counter at Bloomies. Sylvia and Esperanza sniped like a bitter old married couple and freely revealed each other's darkest secrets in strict confidence, but their shared affection was undeniable. And Esperanza could cook.

There they were – whether he was marching into a lion's den, going into battle, or headed for the guillotine, these are the people he wanted by his side. The eight names brought his total with Dale and Zoë to ten. Axel had surprised himself – he thought they were perhaps the finest band of warriors who had ever existed. If he alternated days in which they shared his hell, he would provide them each with fewer than one shitty day a week.

He made a chart with three columns and entitled it "Axel's Death Watch List." Even if he was trying too hard to be funny, at least they would know he was trying. The first column listed names and the second provided contact information. The final column was a sort of Last Will and Testament intended to disperse his meager belongings to the appropriate individuals if he didn't make it. He hoped the last column was just another desperate attempt to be funny.

Then, for the first time since the night of his college graduation party, Axel Hooley dropped his head and sobbed. He swore at whatever God had allowed him to become so ill at 36 . . . or 33, probably, in real years – which was even worse. The alien chemicals departing his body in the flood of tears left his ashen skin streaked with red for most of the next day and infuriated him every time he looked in the mirror.

It occurred to Axel that he was about the same age Christ was when he died, and that idea made his entire existence feel like even more of a debacle. He had accomplished so very little – he had never married, never had children, never even been conclusively in love. He'd never painted a landscape or written a poem or touched another life in any way that enriched it, at least from what he could tell. He had barely even held down a respectable job for any length of time. He wondered if there was enough time left to do anything of value? Depending on what manner of havoc the chemotherapy and radiation wreaked on his reproductive system, children might already be out of the question. And he certainly wasn't any sort of a prize in his current state, so love was no longer on the table either. Not romantic love, certainly. He was too chemo-sodden to do anything creative, and the only job he was currently qualified for was as an experimental guinea pig for medical research. If he died today, his life would have no more effect than the breeze wafting through the trees outside or the moonlight bouncing off the deck.

With his indulgent self-evaluation complete, Axel finally decided to cut himself a little slack. After all, Jesus had been given a pretty clear set of objectives and was far more closely monitored; plus he had a staff of 12, a devoted whore, legions of volunteers, and a mother who didn't dump his ass on the side of the road at the first sign of trouble.

Axel clicked *Send* and blasted the email off to his unsuspecting targets, plus Zoë and Dale. Then he swallowed an OxyContin and floated away, hoping for the best.

# Chapter 7

## Shallow Roots, Widely Placed
## – Part 2

The McKennas weren't merely old hippies, they were old *educated* hippies – the kind that settle in the mountains and eventually achieve tenure at the University of Colorado in Boulder. As they approached their mid-fifties, they certainly didn't think of themselves as old by any stretch of the imagination, and might not even necessarily have owned up to being hippies. In any case, they didn't give a flying fuck what the proprietors of a sad little diner in Tennessee thought of them either way.

Tad McKenna guessed that there was about half a chance the peculiar young lad waiting tables was exactly who he said he was. There was, of course, the very real possibility that Axel – if indeed that was his real name – was one of the smoothest con men the hills had ever known. But Rachel McKenna trusted her instincts, and if the kid wanted to ride along with them for a few hours, she didn't see any harm in it. Wherever they ended up dropping him off would have to be better than where they picked him up. And he seemed so terribly young, despite his dutifully presenting a birth certificate that verified his age as 16.

Childless themselves, the McKennas had made cursory attempts to build their family, but their efforts bore no fruit. They also believed that taking extreme measures in order to replicate themselves in some way would be selfish and imprudent, especially since neither of them felt as if they were missing out on anything. They had their students, after all – legions of them, in fact, over the years. But time whizzes past, and like their trip to see the Great Wall that had never actually manifested, it was a fair certainty that no progeny were in the cards either.

Before long, the academics were both too intrigued and too worried to leave the kid along the way, so they ended up back home in Boulder with Axel ensconced in the large upstairs room that had most recently served as a library. Following what amounted to very little discussion, the McKennas set about doing the only thing they really knew how to do with a young person – educate him.

Every evening, Axel sat at the kitchen table or by the fire in the cozy den with one or both of the McKennas and studied for his upcoming GED test. He quickly realized three essential things: One, his background had prepared him for very little that was of use to the McKennas aside from splitting firewood and preparing a hearty breakfast. Two, he needed to pass his high school equivalency test before he could begin any serious learning. He tried not to dwell on the third and ultimately far more troubling realization – that his future with the McKennas hinged on his ability to prove himself worthy of their time and efforts.

Axel initially thought that Rachel McKenna, the Religious Studies department chair, could be won over by his impressive ability to recite seemingly-endless Bible verses by rote. An expert in Hinduism, Judaism, Buddhism, and Animism, it soon became clear that Rachel was not to be impressed with simple, prosaic Christian memorization. It had never occurred to Axel that there were different points of view on spiritual matters, and in his early days with the McKennas, he hounded Rachel to the point of exhaustion with questions. It seemed completely unreasonable that the identity of God and the origins of man and his soul hadn't been settled once and for all.

When she recognized that Axel had never done any real reading beyond the scripture, Rachel sighed, shook her head, rolled her eyes, and proceeded to the bookshelf, where she thumbed through scores of leather-bound tomes before selecting a dog-eared paperback which she flung toward him.

"What's this?" Axel asked. "Besides some ratty book, I mean?"

Rachel couldn't conceal her smile. "*Valley of the Dolls*. It's absolute trash. I swiped it from my aunt when I was about your age."

"Why is this one better than the others?" Axel asked warily, concerned that Rachel didn't trust him with the more appealing leather-bound volumes.

"Because," Rachel shrugged. "It's chock full of racy bits, and I believe you actually *will* read it."

"Racy bits?"

"*Sex*, Axel. Lots and lots of *sex*." She then proceeded toward her bedroom. "Have yourself a heyday."

"Thanks," he muttered, somewhat embarrassed.

Axel tore through most of it by dawn and learned quite a bit more about the subtleties of seduction than the movies had ever taught him. The highly-charged sexual content delivered as promised and, in fact, transformed Axel into an avid reader overnight.

Tad McKenna was a professor of Environmental Studies, specializing in atmospheric phenomena and ecological management. He and Rachel took Axel hiking in the summer, skiing when it snowed, and taught him the importance of having a passport even if there were no immediate plans for travel.

As it turns out, Axel needn't have worried about his place in the McKenna home. Tad and Rachel had concluded that Axel was a rare find – a blank slate with an eager and curious mind. He was a little backwards of course. That was to be expected, considering his circumstances. He also lacked critical thinking skills, but those were coming, and the McKennas were prepared to provide scores of tutors if that's what was required to jump-start his intellect and maintain his progress. Rachel kept reminding herself that he was so very, *very* young, and once remarked to Tad that if Axel was really 16 years old, she would flap her arms and fly all the way to Denver.

When Axel passed his high school equivalency test, Tad cooked a wonderful celebratory dinner and even served red wine, which Axel didn't much like but drank anyway. The cheerful woozy evening ended with his tearful admission that he was faking his way through life on somebody else's birth record, and what was worse, he was probably a bastard who would never be admitted into the Kingdom of Heaven – so they might as well kick him back into the street right now. Rachel McKenna was extraordinarily touched by the admission and wrapped her arms so tightly around Axel to keep from laughing that her face turned red and tears ran down her cheeks. If they weren't intent on seeing this through up to that point, that was the clincher.

In public, the McKennas blithely referred to Axel as a lodger or an exchange student from Hooterville or Dogpatch if they were feeling particularly clever. To acknowledge anything more would be to admit that their lives had somehow been incomplete without him. Axel very obviously belonged, and he didn't care what other people thought – the three of them understood very clearly their symbiotic and relative importance to one another.

Axel was enrolled at the University and proceeded to sprout up at the startling rate of four inches a year until he reached the height of six feet five inches. He joined the ski team and eventually drew the attention of both the volleyball and soccer coaches, though as it turned out he showed no particular affinity for either sport. Neither Tad nor Rachel would have tolerated the violent nature of football either, so Axel stuck with the ski team and became one of their top performers by his junior year. Tad loved watching Axel on the slopes and believed that the boy resembled something like a tree trying to escape from a mountaintop.

The McKennas saw making the world a better place as part of their job, and they approached the obligation with passion. They protested injustice, valued acumen and the environment, and cultivated friends and colleagues who celebrated all manner of diversity rather than exercising mere tolerance.

Axel accompanied the McKennas on trips to Europe, New York, D.C., and Chicago. He even studied literature in London for a semester, not because of any particular love of literature, but in order to pursue his crush on a skier who eventually led the women's team for the United Kingdom in the Olympics. He couldn't figure out how anybody could learn to ski growing up in Barnsley, but the leggy redhead who shared his flat and his bed had somehow managed it.

Not scholarly by nature, Axel was slow to declare a major, but failure was never offered up as an option so he persevered. He logged more hours at the dining table with one or the other of the McKennas, often under duress, doing his homework and studying. There were tutors when needed, and he eventually declared a major in Sociology because, after all, *everything* felt foreign and strange – why not get a degree for taking a closer look? Axel Hooley was a soul on safari and, as such, was drawn to the ever evolving parameters of civilization and modern culture.

While most college students grow apart from their parents, Axel grew closer to the family he'd stumbled into. The cliché of the college years being among the best of his life held true, but not for the reasons generally cited in alumni newsletters.

The news of the McKennas' deaths was delivered abruptly by the Provost, who had no explicit understanding of their relationship to Axel. They were killed on the autobahn in Germany while Tad McKenna was on his way to lecture in North Rhyne-Westphalia. Axel had wanted very badly to accompany them on the trip, but his final exams prevented him from doing so.

Though most everyone believed it had been the McKennas' wish to include Axel in their Will in some significant way, nobody had taken steps to do so. The son the McKennas loved but never formally acknowledged remained a mere acquaintance in the eyes of the courts. The estate was to be liquidated over the summer to establish a scholarship fund in the McKennas' name.

Axel's many tears were shed quietly and in private. Those who were aware of, or had easily deduced Axel's closeness to the McKennas, offered comfort, but Axel politely demurred and kept to himself. Most of the Boulder natives and University community expected him to behave as if he'd merely lost his landlords, so that's what he did, clinging to the futile hope that being kept at a compulsory distance from the tragedy would make things easier.

In the absence of Tad and Rachel, well-meaning neighbors threw together a last-minute graduation party for him. Axel remembered it as a somber affair where everybody worked too hard coaxing a festive atmosphere that couldn't possibly transpire. Neighbors said it was a shame he wasn't taken into consideration by those in power at the University, but Axel shrugged off such criticism. "I think scholarships are awfully important, too. I'll get along okay." And he reckoned he would somehow muster whatever was necessary to forge ahead – after all, what he had gotten from the McKennas was a lot more valuable than money or real estate.

His foggy plans for graduate school were pushed aside and forgotten. Axel just didn't have the heart for it anymore. He wondered after a while if that future had ever really been his own dream at all, and he didn't see much sense in walking through a door simply because it stood ajar.

In the wee hours following the party, Axel drove the old Jeep Cherokee quietly out of town and wondered if it belonged to him or if he was technically stealing it. He had been driving it for years, but that wasn't any indication of ownership, necessarily. He had definitely stolen a little cash, some jewelry and a few artifacts from the McKenna home, but he didn't think they would mind. He intended to hock the jewelry because funds were running low. Besides, the memories they held made them too painful to keep. And of course Axel didn't need any stupid possessions in order to remember the McKennas.

# Chapter 8

## Vines Entangled

The house was uncharacteristically noisy, but Axel fought the impulse to get up, even though the sunlight creeping through the blinds was triggering his quiescent nausea. The gentle ping announcing the arrival of fresh email every few minutes and the intermittent ringtones of cell phones throughout the house further contributed toward making his battle unwinnable.

He heard Zoë answer her phone at least twice, and the gentle bumping from upstairs indicated that Dale was awake and staggering into things. He heard voices coming from both the living room and outside, or perhaps he was still under the spell of whatever demons had been terrorizing his nights.

Zoë hurried in, texting on her BlackBerry. She shook Axel's leg urgently. "You need to get up."

"I have cancer, bitch. Lay off."

"You have visitors. A *lot* of visitors, in fact. Dale is hiding upstairs." Zoë began pulling at him more aggressively than he thought appropriate for one so delicate and hideously compromised.

Axel opened one eye to see her skirt tucked into the side of her pantyhose. "Visitors? Nobody even knows I'm ..." Axel rolled over and clicked his laptop prompting the screensaver to drop away, revealing 53 email messages. A quick visual scan told him that most were legitimate, non-spam communications. Then he remembered the Death Watch List. "Oh, fuck."

Zoë flung him a pair of fresh sweats, hissed "Hurry!" and scurried out.

Axel's cell phone rang, and he answered with a weary "Hullo?"

Someone sputtered at the other end of the line, then he heard a huff – a very specific and familiar brand of huff. He was searching his memory to pin down its source when the huff repeated itself with more intensity. He definitely recognized it – the reproachful gay huff of utter contempt. That narrowed the field somewhat, probably to Vegas, and most likely to someone he knew through Tommy.

"I am so pissed at you, I don't know what to do."

"Oh. Hi, Damien." Damien was a flight attendant who had dated Tommy briefly before he and Axel fled Las Vegas. Damien was a good guy, though prone to histrionics. "Yeah, sorry." Axel guessed that he was apologizing for having cancer, though he couldn't figure out for the life of him how Damien had heard the news, and he figured he wouldn't have to wait long for the mystery to be solved.

"Some college professor named Millie or Maudie has a Facebook friend who takes a pottery class with my cousin Erica who I brought to see you strip at that dive near the Tropicana back when her husband dumped her."

While Damien's explanation may have been logical, Axel wasn't following. "Huh?"

"Two degrees of separation is the new six degrees. Why wasn't I included on your 'Death Watch' list?"

"Well, I–I–I–" Axel stammered. "You're in Vegas, aren't you?"

Damien huffed again, which prodded Axel toward self-awareness regarding his apparent idiocy. "Right now I'm in Philly, and this afternoon I return to Vegas. But I can go anywhere, you know. *Anywhere!"* Damien's emphasis signified that apparently the outer rings of Saturn were not beyond reach.

"Yes, but you're not here in L.A."

"I can bid one of the Los Angeles routes next month, so I can help take care of you. You can't do this alone. People die, you jackass."

"I'm not going to die, and I'm not alone. Not yet, anyway."

"Do you need anything in the meantime? I have scads of buddy passes if you need to fly to the Mayo Clinic or something, or if there's anybody you need to say goodbye to. You know – just in case." Axel briefly wondered whether Damien was looking to save him or coordinate his farewell tour.

"I'm not supposed to fly. The doctor said." He was thinking in terms of what had or hadn't recently transpired in Beverly Hills rather than his travel options on Jet Blue.

"I have to fly. Call you tomorrow."

Axel clicked his cell phone off and pulled his sweatpants on as quickly as he could, which he thought was still pretty goddamn slow.

He hoped that the shot of Neulasta he received would do the trick and boost his white blood cells back to a reasonable level, because it certainly was making his bones feel old and brittle. A rigorous television campaign for the drug was apparently compelling perfectly healthy people to ask their doctors for Neulasta. The folks in the commercial all looked so healthy and cheerful! Dr. Kenn explained that the sole purpose of Neulasta was to force the bones to produce white blood cells (which Axel thought was a very cool miracle all by its lonesome), but the price for such phenomena was severe body aches bordering on outright agony. Axel certainly had been gifted with the body aches and agony, so he hoped that meant it was working.

Axel didn't know what to expect prior to stepping into the living room, but the beast he'd unleashed the night before had already grown half a dozen heads, all of which turned toward him, jaws agape. Sylvia and Maude stopped mid-conversation on the sofa, and Partho stood in the doorway with a handful of tulips still clinging to their bulbs and dirt clods from whatever garden they were lifted. Rhymey and Esperanza peered out from the kitchen, where Axel imagined the smells of dueling breakfasts were in the air for those still in possession of their olfactory senses.

Zoë turned from the mirror as she was applying her makeup, apparently drawn by the stunned silence echoing through the room. It took Axel a moment to realize that his gaunt appearance was the obvious reason for the awkwardness. He exhaled with a laugh and nodded. "Yeah, I know," he said, which seemed to put them at ease, at least a little. "This *will* get better."

"Of course it will," Sylvia said with a dismissive wave of her hand. "Are you hungry? We brought lox and bagels, and Esperanza is making chorizo."

Rhymey stuck his head out of the kitchen and smiled. "Scrapple will be served too, my brother from another mother!"

Axel leaned on the back of the sofa between Sylvia and Maude so that they could both give him a peck on the cheek. "Step back from the traif, Sylvia – chorizo and scrapple aren't even made out of the *respectable* parts of the pig." Zoë took the tulips from Partho as Axel shambled over and gave him a hug. He had always thought of the boy as small, but Partho lifted Axel in a bear hug and spun him around. "Whoa, dude! Careful." The minimal effort it took not to topple over was exhausting.

Zoë forced the tulips into a nearby urn and made a half-assed attempt to arrange them. "Cheryl called and said she's coming by with her husband tonight. She's bringing brownies."

Maude piped up from the sofa. "And your hunky friend Tyrell went to get orange juice for mimosas."

Axel grinned and shook his head. "Thanks. I almost forgot I was in Los Angeles."

"Mimosas? Great!" Partho plopped into a chair next to Maude.

"Keep junior away from the hooch," Axel muttered as he made his way slowly toward the stairway. If Parth really wanted a party, he should forget about the mimosas and wait for Cheryl's enchanted brownies.

Axel could recall taking Dale's stairs three at a time, but now the idea of plodding up the short flight felt daunting. He considered returning to the den for another OxyContin, but decided to save them for when things really got rough. Three measured steps up, then four, then five, and six. He sat down on the small landing halfway up to recuperate. Half a flight to go. The trip back down would be easier because he could tumble if necessary.

Dale was typing tenaciously on his computer when Axel plodded into his room, and he was not keen to interrupt him. Dale wasn't accustomed to guests without Tommy there to lean on, and Axel didn't know how he was reacting to what had evidently turned into an invitation to dine at his home that he hadn't anticipated.

"You hungry? There's all kinds of food downstairs – Mexican-Amish-Jewish fusion, I think." Dale focused on the computer screen and nodded. He was either angry or concentrating, and Axel couldn't tell which because the wide range of human emotion often looks exactly the same on some of the more stoic Canadians. "If you're not interested in cured salmon or pig snouts and entrails, there will be mimosas. Everybody knows you like to drink." Axel cringed because he meant to sound like he was joking.

After a moment, Dale spoke up, but kept his eyes focused on his computer screen, where he was creating some sort of complex chart. "When you said you needed *help*, your friends must have thought you needed *brunch*."

Axel coughed on a laugh. "Yeah, I guess so. They mean well, they're just . . ." Axel paused, still completely unable to read Dale's mood. "Maybe I should have been more specific?" He wanted to wait as long as necessary for a response, but Axel had always found sustained silence to be agonizing. "Why don't you come downstairs? They're all great people. They take some getting used to maybe, but you'll like them." The tension was starting to get the better of him, and Axel could feel bizarre emotions starting to bubble up. "I asked them for help, and they *came!"* he blurted out, unable to conceal his amazement. *"They just showed up!"*

Dale shrugged slightly, and nodded. "I'll be down in a minute. I want to finish this."

"What are you doing?"

Dale met his gaze. "I'm being more specific. Go."

Axel nodded and backed out of the room, bowing humbly like a serf grateful to have evaded a flogging. Dale didn't seem cross, which was a great relief. Axel had been known to make Dale angry before, typically when he was doing something deliberately irritating like poking him with a stick.

Axel returned to the living room and sat among friends who toasted his health, which was a real laugh riot under the circumstances. Just looking at the scrapple and chorizo was nauseating, but his rescuers had swooped in with encouragement, determination, and mimosas, and he wanted in turn to reward their support by being as tough and amusing as possible. He had never before felt quite so good and quite so dreadful at exactly the same time.

Eventually Dale sailed downstairs, showered and shaved and more handsome than Axel or Zoë had seen him looking in months. He gracefully procured the mantle of host from the various hands quite willing to relinquish it. Introductions were made, and then Dale distributed handouts providing details regarding all of Axel's doctors, the medications Axel was taking including dosage information, and Axel's diet, specifically listing the high-protein foods preferred during the tiny windows of time when he felt like eating.

Axel was astounded at the specificity with which Dale had been guiding his progress. The last document was a sign-up sheet detailing doctors' appointments, his daily radiation schedule, when he was to receive hydration, etcetera. Chemotherapy days were highlighted in yellow. The sheet made the rounds until every transportation slot was called for. Axel would be chauffeured wherever he needed to go whenever he needed to go there.

Axel blinked back tears. He was afraid that if he paused to acknowledge the outpouring of love and concern, he might never stop blubbering. Instead, he focused on his bony feet.

When it was time to leave for radiation, Partho volunteered to take him, mostly so that he could show off his new Porsche. Dale warned that if he took corners too fast or failed to keep his speed in check, Axel would most likely respond in such a way as to quickly eliminate that new car smell and replace it with something notoriously vile and pungent.

They all took turns hugging him goodbye, and he tried to look everyone in the eye as he murmured a quiet "Thank you." There might not be a sufficient opportunity to verbalize his appreciation in the next few months, and he didn't want to fail to do it while he had the chance.

Axel hugged Sylvia last, and felt strength in her hard, determined gaze. As predicted, the feisty octogenarian was tough as a rock. Sylvia Belzer was accustomed to getting what she wanted, and by God she wanted Axel Hooley alive and well and wailing over her casket in another half century or so. She caressed his face before he began the journey down the 93 steps to the street where Partho was parked. "You're so adrift in the world, doll. People don't like that. We worry."

# Chapter 9

## Shallow Roots, Widely Placed
## – Part 3

Axel drove west on I-70 because he had never driven west of Colorado by himself, and the simple act of doing so felt defiant. It was, after all, not possible to be more lost than he already was. He only had a vague grasp of the geography beyond Utah's western border – San Francisco and Los Angeles were out there somewhere, and hopefully there would be traffic signals and good signage to prevent him from absentmindedly wheeling into the Pacific Ocean if he made it that far. His travels with the McKennas had for some reason always taken him east. And anyway, heading into the unknown felt appropriate, so that's what he did.

When I-70 came to an end, he flipped a coin to see which way he should go on I-15 – *tails*, which pointed him south toward Las Vegas. If his quarter had come up heads, it would have led to Salt Lake City and a very different future from the one to be found in Sin City, but that failed to occur to him until later.

The Jeep Cherokee started smoking just beyond the aptly named Valley of Fire State Park and overheated altogether in Gamet, Nevada. He pulled into a service station to let the engine cool and add water. The affable attendant who sold him a bottled green tea and let him use the water hose asked, "Ya headin' ta Vegas?"

Axel nodded but failed to raise much enthusiasm. "Vegas, baby. Yeah." Considering the condition of the Cherokee, he figured Vegas was only about as far as he'd probably get.

Two days after settling into a cheap motel three blocks off the strip, Axel landed a mindless job washing dishes at Vic & Anthony's in the Golden Nugget, but management soon determined him too good looking and well-spoken for back-of-house work, and he began evening shifts as a host. After a month, he transferred to the Grotto, the Nugget's Italian restaurant, and began waiting tables. His schedule was fluid, the tips were good enough, and none of his customers stayed in town long enough to learn his name, which was just fine. After a few months, the chill of the Rockies thawed, Axel warmed up, his disastrous final days in Boulder faded into memory, and he managed to make a few friends.

Axel adjusted to the mind-numbing sameness of everything – the jobs, the tourists, the weather, the sun. The fountains at the Bellagio were stunning to behold on his first day, with their water cannons firing beautiful arcs, spinning streams high into the air, brilliantly choreographed to musical accompaniment – but before long it became just another part of the big phony oasis. After spending his youth engrossed in coerced study in one form or another, the tedium was a welcome relief. He was, for the first time in his life, without anyone to answer to, except for an indifferent shift manager who valued punctuality and reliable attendance above everything else.

After a few months, Axel took an apartment with a young would-be dancer named Tommy who had recently arrived from Chicago. Tommy hoped to get cast in one of the Cirque du Soleil extravaganzas, but ultimately settled for guiding bountiful breast implants across the stage in one of the more traditional "titty & feather" shows. Tommy cited his lack of acrobatic skills, his inadequate upper-body strength, and his inability to swim as reasons the casting deities at Cirque continued to overlook him, and he was determined that a daily regimen of protein and pumping iron would be his ticket to all things fabulous – and *fabulous* was just the right word for Tommy because he was as gay as a feather boa.

Axel accompanied Tommy to the gym mostly out of boredom, and quickly built muscle on top of his already athletic farm boy/ski bum foundation. Tommy's results were more gradual and less pronounced, but he did like the envious glances he got when he arrived and departed with Axel.

The drinking and late nights were fun, but after awhile Axel opted out as often as not. He had grown ever more private since leaving Boulder and took his time confiding in others, including Tommy.

The most well-oiled gears in his wheelhouse – simplicity and education – weren't held in particularly high regard by the locals, and neither would help him secure jobs waiting tables. He felt that if he shared his history with too many people, he wouldn't be able to keep it private and safe. The McKennas specifically were so cherished that he didn't allow himself to dwell on their memory very often or for any length of time, as if doing so might in some way diminish the clarity with which he could conjure them up. So his heart closed and his trusting nature hibernated, but Axel understood this to be temporary because the wind was always changing, and someday he would release the McKennas to the universe and remember who it is they had wanted him to become.

Tommy initially had a chip on his shoulder with regard to his roommate and workout partner, probably because Axel wasn't any more forthcoming with regard to his sexual preference than he was about anything else. Tommy knew there were girlfriends in Axel's past, but figured there wasn't anybody so important as to eliminate the possibility of a little lighthearted experimentation. As Tommy grew closer to Axel, he began to view his friend as a challenge to be conquered, which made their living situation quite untenable, at least as far as Tommy was concerned. Axel wasn't even aware of his potential gay deflowering until Tommy made his move after a particularly raucous night of bar-hopping. Axel was open to the experience, though he didn't approach it with Tommy's enthusiasm, and they quickly reached a point where the whole thing just seemed embarrassing and silly for everybody. Years later, Tommy confided to Dale that it was like seducing some crazy space alien, who approached the process as if it were a kind of science fair project.

Tommy ultimately encouraged Axel, tutored him, and helped him secure a job stripping in one of the lesser-known beefcake shows just off the strip. Tommy readily admitted that he wanted access to all that beefcake, and Axel seemed to be the most direct route toward getting it. The show was small and gimmicky, but Axel moved up to one of the larger venues before long. Tommy helped him develop his various stripper personae – the sexy farm boy, the college jock, and the muscular nerd. He tried "ski bum" a couple of times, but the skis were awkward, and the snowsuit made him all sweaty before he could rip it off; and it felt completely ridiculous in the middle of the desert anyway. His various guises were appealing and approachable, and he often got better tips than the cops and cowboys and construction workers, who he eventually came to refer to as *The Village People*. His face was too innocent and open for him to pull off any of the tougher looks, but he did well with the fiftysomething cougars and the twentysomething hen parties. Business women and well-heeled housewives in their thirties and forties were less receptive and seemed to prefer the more hyper-masculine dancers, but Axel didn't care – he had his niche. Stripping for large groups of women was about the least sexual thing Axel could imagine, and he figured it was very unlike what women endured when stripping for men. The crowds were wild and noisy and drunk and full of laughter, but there was a shared atmosphere of sisterhood that made the whole thing seem more like a celebration than a group grope.

As his official age rounded 23 and headed toward 24, Axel realized his true age must be approaching 21 – finally old enough to frequent the clubs and casinos he'd been working in ever since his arrival three years before. The date signified such a rite of passage in Western culture that Axel wondered if he would be able to feel it when it happened – but of course he never did.

Axel figured this was about as easy as life was going to get – he slept all morning, hit the gym for a few hours, did the show at night, sometimes went out with Tommy and the guys, then back home to sleep until starting the whole cycle again. Axel waited and waited, and six years blew past without a single change in the wind . . .

But when the winds did finally change, so did everything else.

One night in balmy September, Axel joined Tommy and the boys for a late night on the town, when they were attacked in a dark parking lot. The college boys from Texas looked to be part of a football team intent on proving their manhood by beating up a bunch of faggots. And of course as many as half of them actually *were* faggots, but they were faggots who spent the better part of their day at the gym, which was, of course, a dire mistake on the part of the callow, testosterone-charged cowboys.

Everything in Axel's experience taught him that when faced with a fight, the best course of action is always a nonviolent one; so the mêlée of fists and bats was churning all around him before he understood that if he wanted to make it out in one piece, he was going to have to throw a few punches of his own. He took a couple of robust clouts to the face, but quickly learned some key defensive moves that seemed to help.

The strippers, gay and straight alike, were outnumbered by the college boys two to one, but certainly not outmatched. Axel's sheer size discouraged some, who wrongly assumed that the smaller men would be easier marks. As The Village People took care of the final stalwart Texans, Axel spotted Tommy out of the corner of his eye being pursued down the street by two assailants. Tommy was athletic enough, but he wasn't half the size of his pursuers, so Axel lit out after them at full throttle. If they caught Tommy before he caught them, they'd snap poor Tommy like a twig.

Axel sped past the alley where they had dragged Tommy, but quickly realized his mistake and doubled back. He entered the dead end to find one of the thugs holding Tommy's arms behind his back while the other took punches at his face with alternating fists. Axel flushed with adrenaline and white-hot anger – fire breathing rage welled up inside him, fueled by all the injustice of the world – hatred for Carver Twigg and all vicious bullies everywhere, fury at the McKennas for loving him and then dying . . . unmitigated hatred for the disinterested parties that had made him in the first place only to throw him away. The raw emotion burned deeply and felt so unfamiliar that Axel had trouble comprehending exactly what was happening to him.

The gleaming blade of a hunting knife flashed upward in the moonlight, and Axel could see that he was too late. Tommy had dragged him back into the world of the living, while Axel had taken his friendship and all his efforts for granted and kept him at a distance. Now he was going to lose Tommy, and it was his own damn fault for hesitating and not watching out for him the way loyal friends are supposed to. Tommy was going to die at the hands of two drunken college jocks, and there was nothing he could do – no human thing – to save him . . . so Axel Hooley did the only thing he could do, and abruptly lost his mind.

He flew toward Tommy, and with his last tenuous grip on reason, Axel hoped for the best.

# Chapter 10

## Above the Timberline

The cool air blowing on his face was exhilarating. It had been ages since Axel was on the slopes, but the skills had apparently stayed in his body, waiting to be called out. The snow was so fast that he couldn't feel the skis beneath his feet, but it was still invigorating and glorious and remarkably astonishing considering what he'd been up against the past couple of months. The snowpack was always great above the timberline, and Axel reveled in being the first to violate the virgin snow.

Everything had been moving like clockwork, thanks in no small part to the dedication of his trusty friends and Dale's strict adherence to schedule. Everything until that morning, of course, when he had been too ill to go in for radiation and too soggy from the chemo to get in touch with Tyrell to cancel his ride. So when Tyrell got there, he sat down to watch *The View* with Axel and bicker over which of the assorted bitch-fest hostesses they'd least like to fuck. After Tyrell left, Axel realized he had forgotten to invite Tyrell to join him on the slopes. Tyrell would have loved this, and he felt sad that his friend was missing out.

It seemed outrageous that he could be up on skis already . . . How was that even possible? Maybe he was on a bobsled instead? Still, the fresh air felt good, and he loved being outside in the elements, assuming of course that he didn't catch pneumonia in his depleted state. What irresponsible dolt had allowed him out on the slopes in his condition anyway? It was the fourth day of his five-day chemotherapy infusion, and day four always set off a whole host of difficulties from erratic fevers to neutropenia.

Dale was at a meeting in Santa Barbara with a new client, so Esperanza had come by around 11:00 and brought some ginger root tea to settle his stomach, but it didn't work, and he wasn't able to eat the ample meal she lugged up to the house either. So instead, he sprawled out on the sofa and watched a telenovela with her. He didn't understand much of it, but of course he hadn't fully comprehended *The View*, either. Maybe he was running a fever?

After Esperanza left, he went into the kitchen to nuke some of the ginger tea and maybe try to force down a couple of vanilla wafers. Everything tasted like cardboard, but he felt like he should eat something. Dale's ceramic mug from a *Sons of Maxwell* concert slipped through his fingers and shattered on the tile, splashing tea everywhere, which was going to make Dale none too happy. He couldn't very well leave the mess, so he got a fresh roll of paper towels from the pantry and sat on the kitchen floor to pry the package open. It was good to relax. Axel found that if he laid down on the tile, it felt nice and cool on his feverish face, and the roll of paper towels made a superb teddy bear.

Being strapped to a bobsled seemed like a really shitty idea too, and Axel couldn't for the life of him figure out who thought of it. It was really more like a luge than a bobsled anyway, and maybe that's how it was done? He had never actually been on one before. He wanted to puke, but there was nothing in his stomach, and it seemed that lashing him to a luge and sending him zigzagging downhill was somehow mean-spirited and completely wrong. Whoever was responsible should probably be struck from his Death Watch List. Maybe this was some kind of aggressive therapy, like a zippy little hyperbaric chamber or something?

Maude had come by that afternoon, apparently to yell at him in some foreign tongue. All he could make out was "Bleah-bleah-bleah Dale called and said bleah-bleah-bleah-bleah," and "Answer me! Bleah-bleah-bleah-bleah-bleah!" Axel just wanted her to shut the hell up, clean up Dale's broken mug, and leave him in peace.

Axel had been in possession of just enough wherewithal to identify the two men as paramedics when they arrived, but he was too exhausted to care who they had come for. He just wished they would stop pawing at him. He didn't put up a fight when they strapped him to the gurney, and was just able to make out a hasty discussion about how to navigate the contraption down the hill to the ambulance.

The chemo-clouds briefly parted, and it all suddenly flashed clear – Axel wasn't on skis or a bobsled or even a luge – he was strapped to a wheeled gurney racing down Sunset Boulevard toward what would surely be imminent death. The gurney must have slipped out of the grip of the paramedics as they made their way down the treacherous steps leading from Dale's house to the street below. He managed to reconstruct a jumbled memory of careening down onto Hamilton Way, sloping onto Westerly Terrace, blowing through the stoplight, and veering onto Sunset Boulevard. The gurney obviously had an agenda, like water seeking its own level.

So he knew where he was and where he was headed, but in this instance knowledge did not bestow much power. Axel squeezed his eyes shut and tried to thrust his weight toward the right. He trusted that he would roll to a stop in the bike lane sometime before Sunset became Cesar Chavez Avenue and hoped that he would do so before he got run down by traffic.

If this was how it was supposed to end, Axel prayed that those he left behind would at the very least come to appreciate the hilarity of the whole thing.

# Chapter 11

## Two Tumbleweeds

Axel heard someone screaming from far away. The voice gradually drew closer until he could hear Tommy's shouts. "Stop it, Axel! You'll kill him! Axel! Stop!" He turned and blinked at Tommy who was curled up into a ball and cowering against a dumpster. As Axel's fury subsided, he abruptly stopped what he was doing, which turned out to be punching the face of a stranger into a bloody pulp.

He couldn't seem to make contact with what exactly had driven him to such a repulsive act, but Axel sensed that he could beat the unconscious man to death and might still burn with unspent rage. So he smashed him in the teeth one last time and flung him to the ground.

Axel reached out toward Tommy, who scuttled away terrified. Another man sprawled near Tommy, unconscious, with one arm twisted at an alarming angle. Something terrible had happened in the alley, and some of it had obviously happened to Tommy. Axel looked back at the man he had been hitting – his face was smashed and bloody, and his right hand was a smoldering stump with steam rising off it.

Axel shook his head to clear it, but still felt disoriented. It took a moment to find his voice. "What happened to his hand?" Tommy didn't respond, so Axel turned and insisted. "Well?"

"It . . . It melted," Tommy squeaked.

"It *melted?*" Axel wasn't certain Tommy was even speaking English. "Are you okay?" Tommy nodded, but was obviously frightened and didn't take his eyes off Axel. Axel realized suddenly that the thing Tommy was terrified of was him. Axel knelt gently and asked again. "You okay?" Axel could tell by looking that Tommy would be alright – nothing truly awful was going to happen to Tommy for another seven years, ten months and four days. The strange thought startled him and only added to his confusion, so he quickly pushed it aside, where it abruptly vanished.

Axel glanced around the alley to see if there was anybody else he hadn't noticed. The man lying near Tommy obviously had a broken arm, but didn't seem to be in dreadful shape otherwise. The bodybuilder with the bludgeoned face and the smoldering hand was another story, however. He needed medical attention and he needed it fast, so Axel threw him over his shoulder and ran six long blocks to North Vista Hospital, where he pitched him through the open door of the emergency room and then bolted.

When Axel hurtled back into the alley, Tommy looked up with a start from where he was poking the unconscious man with the toe of his sneaker. "Where did you go?" he asked, timidly.

"I dropped him at the emergency room."

"You were only gone a minute," Tommy managed to croak. "Not even that long."

Axel flopped onto the ground and leaned against the dumpster, reminding himself to move slowly to keep from startling Tommy. He took deep breaths and tried to slow the thunderous pounding of his heart. "So, what happened?" Tommy was studying him suspiciously, and Axel was getting impatient. "I'm sorry, but I don't know. Did I hurt you? Did *they* hurt you?"

"I'm alright, I think." Tommy was almost convinced Axel was telling the truth. Was it possible he really didn't remember?

"Fuck this. We're going home." Axel scooped Tommy up before he could object and carried him out to the street where he hailed a cab. They stopped only briefly so that Axel could run into a 7-Eleven and anonymously call for an ambulance to pick up the man with the broken arm in the alley.

Tommy kept his eyes trained on Axel as he carried him into the bathroom, sat him down and began carefully cleaning his wounds with alcohol swabs. Tommy had been living under the assumption that he knew Axel like he knew his own soul, and he believed there was not a fiber of the tall man's being that wasn't infused with gentleness. What he thought he had seen simply was not possible – not for Axel – not for anybody. The world felt more normal with each passing moment, and for the sake of his sanity, Tommy gradually convinced himself that he had imagined the whole thing. He'd been punched awfully hard, after all, so he never brought it up again. Not to Axel anyway, though he did eventually recount the wild tale to Dale years later after they'd had a particularly trying day with Axel.

Tommy felt like he should say something, but wanted to forget the terrible events at hand. What he came out with surprised them both. "My parents threw me out when I told them I was gay. A high school friend lived out here already, so I slept on her floor for a month while I decided what to do. I told you I moved here to audition for Cirque du Soleil because it sounded less pathetic."

Axel's eyes danced as he feigned surprise. "My God! You're *gay?*" Axel winced along with Tommy as he wiped clean a gash on his eyebrow. Axel was cornered, so he relented and offered a nugget of his own. "My parents dumped me when I was a little kid. I don't even remember them."

Tommy nodded and fought back tears, though he wasn't certain what exactly they were honoring with their appearance.

"And my next set of folks put me on a bus out of town when I was barely a teenager because I wasn't Amish enough for them, and probably wasn't ever gonna be." As the flood gates officially opened, Axel felt relief wash over him.

Tommy guffawed with surprise and began to rethink how well he actually *did* know Axel. "My God! You're *Amish?*"

"You've heard of 'Black Irish?' I'm sort of 'Black Amish.'"

"Holy shit! You win!" Tommy laughed so hard that he started choking, and he couldn't believe he had been afraid of his friend and defender just moments before. The heightened emotion of the night prompted Tommy and Axel to spill their respective histories, and by daybreak Tommy was the closest thing Axel would ever have to a brother.

Tommy confessed that he had wanted to move to Los Angeles when he left Chicago, but the best he could do was get to Las Vegas. He thought maybe he would like to work at a film or television studio or do some kind of production work.

Axel shrugged casually. "Why don't we do it, Tommy? We can go to Los Angeles right now."

Tommy was both intrigued and frightened of the idea. "But we just got home, and we haven't slept. You've barely had time to jiggle the crumpled singles out of your underpants."

Axel grinned impishly as he dragged his suitcases out of the closet. "I'll shake the change out at a rest area – you might need quarters for the soda machine."

Tommy regretted bringing the whole L.A. thing up, even if it really was the perfect time and the perfect place to go. But Axel was already on the move, and Tommy wasn't entirely convinced that his loyal friend the Amish stripper wasn't a force of nature, so he went along with it. As he packed his things, he found that he shared Axel's enthusiasm for the harebrained plan.

As far as Axel was concerned, a change was long overdue, and he didn't want the gusto train to pass them by. The thought of exploring Los Angeles (or anyplace else) was exciting. Besides, they could drive it in just a few hours, and the idea of actually going somewhere *with* somebody was appealing.

Tommy took the first shift behind the wheel, but ended up driving all the way to Los Angeles because Axel fell asleep in the passenger seat and couldn't be roused from slumber for nearly

17 hours. After all that had happened, Tommy wasn't a bit surprised.

They spent their first night in Los Angeles in the parking lot of the In-N-Out Burger on Sunset between Highland and La Brea. They soon came to understand this to be one of the most well-lit, crowded and noisy late-night locations in the entire city, but they were so exhausted that the commotion didn't bother them. They were together, and for now, wherever they found that to be, was home.

# Chapter 12

## In the Shade of the Mighty Oak

Music drifted through the branches from just beyond the hill. Rugged. Unsophisticated. Ancient. Celtic, maybe? He realized that he was dreaming, for whatever that was worth. He floated high above a village square where ruddy-faced, fun-loving peasants came and went and worked and danced and fell in love and propagated and grew old and feeble and died. A strange sort of kinship pulsated between them and himself – an entirely new sensation that defied description, though he clearly recognized his presence as completely separate from theirs. He was not one of them, yet felt connected in the same ways as the land and the sky.

The villagers were generally peaceful, though they often drank too much and brawled every now and again. They loved their families and treated their animals and their land with respect. They celebrated and mourned, passed down love and knowledge from generation to generation, and he observed it all, perched somewhere just beyond reach. There seemed a sense of inevitability about their lives that was punctuated constantly by the most surprising incidents and unexpected episodes.

A violent storm gathered in the distance. It might have been frightening, but he felt it was just another part of everything else, like the seasons.

Axel coughed and sat up, suddenly wide awake. He blinked at Claude and Cheryl Vogel, who looked startled. "Where am I?"

"You're at Cedars-Sinai, sweetie," Cheryl whispered. "Private room. Very nice. Sexy nurses. How do you feel?"

"Pretty good, actually." Axel felt better than he had in weeks, in fact. Peaceful, yet completely plugged in.

"You should be feeling damn good," Claude chortled. "Nurse Goodbody just gave you four cc's of Dilaudid."

Cheryl giggled in agreement. "That'll give ya more bing-bang-boom than anything I can whip up in my little country kitchen, I tell ya what! Which reminds me . . ." She took what looked like a plastic bread wrapper out of her bag and tucked it into the drawer of Axel's side table, whispering discreetly. "I made brownies. Have the nurse heat 'em up if you can – it'll help activate the THC."

"How long have I been out?"

"Off and on a coupla days," Claude shrugged. "Zoë and Whatzis went down to the cafeteria. We're keepin' ya comp'ny 'til the shrink gets here."

Claude took an elbow to the ribs from Cheryl, who followed up with a big slap to his leg.

"I have to see a shrink?" Axel asked, raising what he figured were his eyebrows, even if there were no longer any hairs up there.

"It's surely standard procedure, Axel," Cheryl assured him. "They gotta keep pokin' at ya so ya won't fall in love with your pain meds!"

As if on cue, a bouncy, cheerful young woman with a sunbeam for a smile stuck her head in the door. "So which one of you is Axel Hooley?" None of them immediately owned up to it, possibly because they weren't certain she was joking, so she solved the mystery on her own. "I'm Melissa Freeman." She stuck her hand out to Axel, who chose instead to wave. In his depleted state, he wasn't eager to acquire whatever germs Melissa may have picked up with her warm salutations. "Can we have a little chat?"

Cheryl and Claude stood and moved toward the door. "We gotta get back to the clinic anyway," Claude said.

Cheryl nodded in agreement. "If we're gone too long, the customers get itchy." They waved and left before Axel could even register a protest. Axel thought the shrink looked to be in her early twenties. Certainly not much older. If she'd had long sausage curls, she could probably pass for a teenage refugee from some well-to-do family in a Dickens novel.

"First off, Axel, let me give you something you might find useful."

Melissa reached into her vinyl shoulder bag and pulled out a folder, which she opened and placed on his lap. A pamphlet sporting a *Death & Dying* headline fell out of the folder, which Axel couldn't imagine was what she intended. Axel opened it up to find Elisabeth Kübler-Ross's *"Five Stages of Dying"* outlined in a comforting, large, Times New Roman font – with italics, intended no doubt to further cushion the blow: *Denial, Anger, Bargaining, Depression, Acceptance.*

Axel gazed at the pamphlet a moment, then looked up. "So Ms. Freeman . . . You're the shrink?"

"We like the term *therapist*," she said.

"Okay. So why do I need a therapist?"

"I'm not actually a therapist. I'm more of a social worker, really."

"Why do I need a social worker, Ms. Freeman?"

"*Everybody* needs a social worker. And you can call me Melissa. Or Missy, if you prefer."

Axel nodded and repeated her name. "Missy." He hated being alone with her because Missy was shaping up to be comedy double platinum, which was completely useless without an audience. "So you're my assigned 'Death Therapist?' Or 'Death *Social Worker?*'" Axel self-corrected.

"Between you, me, and the wall, I'm kind of an intern," Missy confided in a broadly comical vaudevillian aside.

"They gave me a Death *Intern?*"

"I'm highly skilled in the practice area," she chirped. "And you don't have good insurance, so beggars can't be choosers." Missy sounded as if she was concealing some embarrassment, so Axel decided to give her the benefit of the doubt, though for some reason he felt as if he were caving in to pressure from a suspiciously slick telemarketer.

Missy settled into a chair as Axel formulated questions in his mind, which turned out not to be necessary because she already had her own list of checkpoints.

"I'm technically not supposed to be talking to the terminally ill just yet, but they say I'm a go-getter."

"I'm terminally ill?" Axel blinked. "Who says I'm terminal? Nobody told me anything about being—"

"Don't worry," she giggled as she patted his shoulder. "Nobody ever tells me anything. I just calls 'em as I sees 'em." Missy winked in a way that made Axel suspect that she may have heard something specific.

"Well, Missy," Axel said in a measured tone, still wondering what to make of her. The last thing he wanted to sound like was a crotchety invalid. "I'm not dying just yet. And secondly, I don't see any reason to plan for it, either way."

"When we fail to plan, we plan to fail!"

Cancer had made Axel sore and irritated and confused, and never in his life had he been more in need of someone to bitch-slap. All his friends, caregivers, and the gentle doctors and nurses who had committed themselves to helping him fight the hateful disease were not suitable, appropriate, or desirable targets, however. Up until now, Axel's only hope was that a clueless or inconsiderate stranger might happen onto his path. Axel very badly wanted to massacre Missy and her fortune-cookie wisdom, preferably in such a way that would slaughter her loved ones for bonus points. Missy opened the Death & Dying pamphlet, her body exhibiting outward signs of an impending squeal of delight.

"*Denial* is the first step in your journey, in fact!" she said as she patted his shoulder and winked. "You can think of me as your transitional guide."

Axel felt the last rubber band on his self-restraint snap. "You don't just tick off these stages on some checklist, and then we're done, you dumb bitch!"

Missy pursed her lips and nodded repentantly. Then she winked at him again and whispered "Stage two – *Anger*."

Axel felt as if he'd been robbed. The two best trump cards in the cancer deck were rage and tears. She had robbed him of the former, and he wasn't about to surrender the latter, at least not to a dipshit like Missy.

"I need to speak with Dr. Kenn," he said, through gritted teeth.

Missy looked wounded. "Why do you need Dr. Kenn? Are you feeling poorly?"

"Yes, I'm feeling poorly," Axel said, though he wasn't certain Missy could tell he was restating the obvious.

"I'll see if I can find him as soon as we're done."

"I need to see him *now*," Axel insisted. "After I talk to him, then you and I can finish our little death march. Okay?"

Missy looked as if she'd hit the jackpot. Her eyes widened, and that irritating sunbeam spread across her face once again. She pointed reverently to number three on the Kübler-Ross list and whispered *"Bargaining,"* ever so gently.

Axel was losing his battle of wits with a ditzy coed who had initially appeared to be unarmed. He had never been so far off his game or so underestimated an adversary. What if his cleverness never came back? What if the innumerable other things seeping away never found their way back? What then? He rolled away from Missy and moaned. "Leave me alone, please. Just leave me alone and let me die."

Missy squealed and clapped her hands. *"Depression!* Oh, good for you, Axel! We've only got one more."

Axel turned to face Missy, holding his hands up in surrender. Fighting her was too much. "I give up. You win. I bow to your superior skill, knowledge, and understanding of everything that matters. I'm dead. I'm done."

Missy heaved a sigh of relief and tossed the pamphlet onto the bed. "Whew! Number five – *Acceptance*. There you go! I can't believe they told me this was gonna be hard."

"So what else is in your folder?" Axel asked, not that he was interested.

"We covered everything that's really important," Missy grinned. "The rest is just rubbish you won't need to bother with – survivor programs and follow-up treatment and such." Missy pitched the folder into the trash.

Axel smirked and held her gaze. "What makes you so sure I'm a goner, Missy?" He couldn't help but ask, despite the risk of opening up yet another can of ringworms.

"Well, I mean . . ." Missy scanned his body up and down with her eyes. "*Come on!*"

Her honesty was oddly refreshing. "Don't put too much stock in how I look," Axel assured her. "When I don't have cancer, I'm totally hot."

"Oh, you are?" Missy smiled, sounding surprised. "I mean . . . Sure you are, Axel! That's the spirit!"

"You're gonna have to trust me. If I were at the top of my game, you'd be totally damp down there."

Missy just smiled and crinkled her brow. Axel could tell she hadn't yet given much thought to anything that may or may not be going on below her waist. He hoped that some drunken night Missy would fall head over heels for a Hell's Angel or maybe a militant lesbian with something to prove – some wildly inappropriate romance or tragic heartbreak – anything that might totally upend her world view. In the long run, it would help facilitate her transformation into the caring, thoughtful archangel she already perceived herself to be.

"Look, Missy," Axel smiled. She had vanquished him fair and square. Perhaps he could turn his foe into an ally. "I agree that I might need to talk to somebody. In fact, there are a lot of things happening to me that I'm having trouble understanding. But I would rather speak to somebody about how to survive rather than how I might go about dying."

Disappointment wrote itself across Missy's face in a large, legible font – Times New Roman with italics. "But we've struggled to get you to stage five – *Acceptance*. Why would you want to go and undo all our hard work?"

"Oh, *acceptance* is right here waiting for me, whenever I need it," Axel assured her. "But if I'm going to die, it's going to happen whether I'm ready for it or not, isn't it?"

"But . . . wouldn't you rather be prepared?"

Axel didn't need to think about it. "Not at all. I like surprises." And that was probably a good thing because Axel had been surprised at every turn of every corner for as far back as he could remember.

"I'm more interested in life than death, at least for right now. If I'm going to live – and I'm not saying that I will, mind you – I might as well use the time to get some things figured out. Right?"

"I suppose so." Missy seemed devastated that he hadn't begun designing his tombstone. "What kind of person would you prefer to talk to?"

"Somebody who knows about chemical changes in the body or someone who can help untangle my muddled dreams, maybe? I'm not sure. Perhaps I just need somebody with a little more experience." Axel rolled it around in his head a minute, but couldn't rephrase it in any way that wasn't condescending. "Someone really wise who might be able to help me sort some things out." He paused one last time. "Definitely not a candy striper."

"Okay, Axel," Missy nodded thoughtfully. "Let me see what I can do." She left Axel's room looking a little sad. Axel felt bad for her, although he remained convinced that Missy had never successfully sorted out anything, except perhaps socks.

# Chapter 13

## Hollywood and Environs

Axel and Los Angeles were a surprisingly good match, possibly because they both came without much history. The chronicle of Hollywood was the history of film and television and little else, after all, and only harkened back just over a century. Historically speaking, not even the blink of an eye. Axel could wrap his arms around Hollywood and embrace the one place where he didn't need to feel insecure about his lack of pedigree. Everyone in L.A. came from somewhere else, and most were inventing their stories as they went along.

The first thing Axel said upon waking in the parking lot of the In-N-Out Burger, was "Let's go surfing." He didn't know why he said it, or even that he wanted to do it before that moment, but it seemed like the thing to do in California. So he and Tommy drove to Santa Monica, rented a couple of surfboards, and set about trying to drown themselves.

They settled into a somewhat run-down hotel near the beach and took a crash course in hang gliding after being wait-listed for a surfing course. The aptly named *Crash Course* consisted mostly of leaping off a twelve foot sea cliff strapped into a hang glider and either gently gliding or awkwardly crashing onto the beach below. After two weeks, it occurred to Axel and Tommy that nobody was going to pay them to surf or hang glide no matter how skilled they became, so they were probably going to need jobs and perhaps even a more permanent place to live. Axel didn't know what he was going to do for work, but he promised himself that it wouldn't involve taking his clothes off for money.

Tommy suggested that they get a place in Hollywood, but he only knew the iconic locale from its press coverage, and Hollywood had a public relations machine that was obviously far too effective. The true Hollywood turned out to be just a regular neighborhood within Los Angeles, and not an always desirable neighborhood at that. West Hollywood and Beverly Hills were their own separate, unique, and official cities, side by side and entirely pleasant, surrounded by Los Angeles on their remaining sides. The San Gabriel Valley and the San Fernando Valley were also technically Los Angeles, though the San Fernando Valley kept threatening to secede every few years. The San Fernando Valley was also widely known for the making of pornography, while the San Gabriel Valley generally housed suburban families and was alleged to harbor a few semidetached meth labs. And anyway, they ultimately didn't come to the city to live in the hinterlands, so they limited their search to the L.A. basin. Santa Monica and Venice provided excellent beach access and were, therefore, out of their price range. Culver City was run down in places, and experiencing a renaissance in others that somehow felt desperate. Century City was too full of high-rises, and several otherwise acceptable neighborhoods were marred by numerous strip malls, which reminded them too much of Vegas.

Tommy preferred West Hollywood, or "Weho," because he liked the gay rainbow-emblazoned city insignia on the police cars, but they settled on a studio apartment in Beverly Hills instead because it was technically not a legal residence, and therefore comparatively cheap. Besides, it provided them with a trendy address, and Axel liked the spirited, elderly landlady, Mrs. Beatrice Klepford, who always asked that everybody call her "Bea," although nobody ever really did. Axel called her "Aunt Bea," however, because the sweetness of their relationship made Tommy gag.

Axel intuitively felt that his time with Tommy was coming to an end, whatever that was going to mean, and the studio apartment with the window shaded by a large elm would be the perfect place for him once Tommy moved on. Axel felt a growing, uneasy sense of destiny with Tommy that he didn't sense with anybody else, as if they were to do something profound and life-altering together. Axel understood he had a role to play in whatever was to happen, but Tommy seemed poised to move forward on his own. So Axel set about picking the appropriate time and circumstances to kick his fledgling out of the nest. Tommy would have disagreed with regard to who was the fledgling and who would kick, so Axel kept quiet about the whole thing and surreptitiously set about trying to find a partner for Tommy. If left to his own devices, Axel shuddered to imagine the cretinoid Tommy might end up with. Tommy was easily blinded by what Axel believed to be superficial qualities, which were particularly dangerous when artfully paraded by the skillful Weho homo.

Axel considered himself a far better judge of character than Tommy, and proved it one night when they went clubbing. After their years in Vegas, Axel was not a fan of trendy night spots, let alone the rough-and-tumble gay bar scene in Silverlake, but he knew that Tommy liked to use him as bait, so he put on a clean, white wifebeater and went along for the ride.

Dale was exactly the sort that Tommy wouldn't have glanced at twice if Axel hadn't turned his head in Dale's direction. Axel introduced himself to Dale, chatted him up, forged a friendship, and hung in there long enough for Tommy to come around and realize what a true prize Dale really was. To Tommy's credit, it only took about a month. And to Dale's benefit, he went along with it, because falling for Tommy wasn't difficult. After two months of power dating, Tommy flew the coop and moved to Silverlake where he and Dale began feathering their nest.

Axel found a part-time job installing cabinetry in the kitchens of the well-to-do and the very, *very* rich throughout Beverly Hills, Westwood, and Bel Air. He was easygoing and gregarious when that seemed like the thing to be, and kept to himself and worked quietly whenever it was required, which turned out to be only very rarely. The elegant homes sheltered a lot of stay-at-home spouses and wealthy executives and celebrities who were bored to tears and seemed grateful for the beguiling attention of a well-spoken handyman who was proficient in English. Axel was fascinated by the hopes, dreams, thoughts, and affairs people secretly harbored, yet willingly revealed to a transitory stranger.

Axel quickly learned that both time and money behaved differently in Los Angeles than anywhere else. He would wave goodbye to someone and shout "Let's have lunch next week," and then a year would flash by before they'd meet again. And the money made and lost in La La Land and the brief amount of time it took to go from one to the other was absolutely staggering.

There seemed no sort of reliable formula to predict how ready cash would behave in any individual's hands, and everyone appeared to be on their way toward getting a big pile of it, or losing every dime. Axel hailed from worlds considered to be meritocracies – if you worked hard and stayed on track, you got ahead and were thusly rewarded, or at least that's how it was supposed to work. Los Angeles was more of an aristocracy – fame, money, and adulation were awarded and withdrawn based on the flimsiest and most nonexistent of criteria: the arbitrary timing of chance events, accidents of birth, physical beauty (whether provided by nature or the scalpel), making the right connection at the right moment or not, and any number of other uncontrollable elements.

Axel soon came to appreciate the ways he himself had been shaped by the randomness of the world, which, of course, further confirmed L.A. as the perfect home.

After almost a year, Axel enrolled in massage therapy school, which he attended for about six months before dropping out. Tinseltown was not a place that necessarily required a degree, assuming that you didn't intend to practice medicine or law, and even the rules governing medicine were locally fuzzy. L.A. was a place where further training could be obtained on the job, and the jobs were there.

Axel had strong hands and a bag of toys if he needed them and could provide a "happy ending" for anybody, of either sex, who asked for one, assuming they tipped accordingly. While the release was plainly a sexual moment for the client, it certainly wasn't the case for Axel, who felt that the generous tips were the only thing preventing him from spending more time installing kitchen cabinetry.

He didn't know if this was a step up or a step down from stripping, but he eventually decided not to make any more of it than it was – a simple business transaction for services rendered. And he had plenty of legitimate clients who just wanted a relaxing rubdown because a massage is sometimes *just* a massage.

When push came to shove, Axel didn't see much difference between installing a retired couple's kitchen cabinets, giving a carb-starved starlet a soothing massage, or whacking off a stressed-out studio executive. People were generally pleasant and grateful and nearly always complimented him on his craftsmanship.

Axel liked being out in the city every day and easily forged relationships, many of which stood the test of time. He wasn't conscious of building a network, and it never occurred to him that there might someday be a need to assemble his own safety net. People were easy to like and fun to be with, and the ones with the warmest hearts usually found ways to make themselves known.

Sylvia had been a cabinetry-installation client, as had Zoë, though he met Zoë the first time when one of her sorority sisters had referred him for a massage. Four days later, when he arrived at her house to install kitchen cabinets, Axel was grateful she hadn't asked for anything more complicated than a standard massage.

The truly outstanding and complex relationships, like those with Zoë and Dale, took a bit longer to forge because they needed more tending than the common garden-variety friendships. Assuming you hadn't survived some catastrophe or natural disaster together, it was best just to keep at it and let things unfold however they were supposed to.

Axel and Zoë managed to end up in bed together one night during their first few months of friendship, but Axel hadn't fared much better with Zoë than he had with Tommy, all previous indications of a successful pairing aside. They already cared about each other deeply, but ultimately collapsed under the weight of their own expectations.

When they finished, or rather, abandoned the coupling process, they lay in bed quietly until Zoë finally broke the uncomfortable silence. "I think that chemical attraction isn't necessarily the best method of selection with regard to permanency."

Axel sighed with relief. "I think sex is kind of a joke our hormones play on us, when you think about it. It blinds us to anything that might be interpreted as a flashing yellow light warning us that it's friendship we're probably supposed to be having."

"So we're done with this?" she asked, hesitantly, then proceeded to make the decision for herself. "I'm done, anyway. So if you're done, I'm done."

Axel nodded, a little sadly. "Yeah, I'm done." They lay there for a long moment, not even touching. "I liked falling in love with you, though."

Zoë guffawed audibly and gave him a playful swat. "You didn't fall in love, Axel! Not really."

"Yeah, Zo. I think I did, a little bit." Axel seemed to be concentrating, so she let him be, understanding that he would come out with it if he formulated a conclusion worth sharing. "I think maybe when we fall in love with someone, we can't see them anymore – what we see is ourselves reflected in the best possible light, and it's totally intoxicating and completely addictive. And for some reason, I can't seem to make that kind of passion last."

"Me, neither," Zoë added, somewhat surprised that Axel had been able to so succinctly sum up feelings she didn't even know she had.

"Maybe passion is too easy?" Axel sighed drowsily, as he snuggled in and held Zoë's hand close to his heart. "Passion can be conjured up with any number of folks for a lot of silly reasons. It's all these stupid little moments that rush past without us noticing that I think are probably the really important things."

It seemed unlikely to Zoë that Axel was capable of conceptualizing and articulating definitive insight with regard to passion, unobserved moments, and the genuine nature of love, but she tucked it away to think about later. "Maybe. Right or wrong, I suppose there are a lot of very good reasons why some of us end up with a lot of great friends and no lifelong romantic partners."

Axel smiled. "It's easy for some people, I think. But for the rest of us, finding the right one is like trying to find the unicorn in the forest."

Having examined, dissected, and driven a wooden stake through the heart of their hours-old romance, they got up in the morning, threw the sheets into the wash, and spent the rest of the day on the Santa Monica Pier, eating corn dogs and laughing at their own ridiculousness. Just as with Tommy, Axel was relieved to have wrung all romantic possibility out of the relationship so that they could proceed and actually become whatever meaningful thing they were supposed to be with each other.

Sex still held the same fascination it had during Axel's adolescent years, but the tentacles and unbridled emotion that accompanied it were so baffling that it just didn't seem to be worth the trouble. Axel figured he would get around to dealing with all of that at some point. In the meantime, those who continued to share his days were so brilliant and astonishing that he couldn't imagine compromising it all in favor of focused affection from any one individual. As for the preference issue, Axel suspected maybe he was straight, at least by statistical and sociological standards, but he didn't really give a damn one way or the other.

He hung out with Tommy and Dale a great deal, and only occasionally felt like a third wheel. Dale was never anything but gracious about Axel's semiregular and relentless company at their dinner table. Axel was aware by now that his ongoing presence could be trying, but he was clueless as to how to go about politely extracting himself from the relationship. Not everybody had the patience for his attempts to sort out the world, often at length, and usually out loud, nor his clumsy efforts to draw useful, meaningful assumptions about anything. Dale's efforts to distill large concepts down into simple, bite-sized terms only seemed to complicate things. Dale and Tommy agreed that tossing pearls of wisdom into the murky waters of Axel's psyche only made ripples and churned up more murk.

Axel's friendship with Tommy was never forced or anything but effortless, yet he couldn't shake the feeling that they were only biding their time together, waiting for something unavoidable to happen.

# Chapter 14

## Tied to a Tree

Axel didn't want to get sick in Partho's Porsche, but if they didn't stop soon, he might not have a choice. His churning stomach had not yet indicated whether he would be throwing up or experiencing the dreaded and far-worse alternative, but something was going to happen and soon.

Partho was probably cutting class in order to chauffeur him around, but reprimanding him did little good. The kid always insisted that he was way ahead in school, which was probably true. It would be interesting to see how eager a cabbie he would be after Axel ruined his custom seat covers.

"You okay?" Partho asked, sharing Axel's sense of dread.

Axel concentrated on breathing.

"If you're gonna hurl, I can pull over. Just say the word."

"I'm not gonna hurl," Axel assured him, which in this case was less than comforting. "Just go, speed racer."

Partho zoomed west on Santa Monica Boulevard past Wilshire and away from Beverly Hills and the last wooded patch that might provide some measure of camouflage should the battle now relocate to his intestines and decide to go nuclear. Axel had managed to foul himself in front of just about everyone at one time or another in recent weeks, but he desperately wanted to spare Partho the full fireworks display. Dale had quietly purchased Axel a package of adult diapers, but wearing them was demeaning, and he never seemed to have one on when he really needed it.

By the time they pulled into the high-rise where Axel was to meet his new therapist, he knew it might be too late. He watched as Partho took the ticket from the parking machine and the gate swung up in comical slow motion. Partho spun quickly around the corner and shot into a parking space as Axel threw the door open and rolled out onto the cement in his frenzy to get his sweatpants pulled down. His next few moves were key, and he managed to execute them without annihilating either his clothes or the car, which is a lot more than could be said for the wall of the parking structure. He hoped the trendy Century City high-rise had a hazmat team at the ready; otherwise, the whole place was going to have to be condemned.

Partho guffawed with horror and amazement. "Migod! You totally, totally crapped!"

"How about you show a little discretion and look the other way?!" Axel sputtered. "And see if you can find me some tissue."

Axel freshened up in the lobby restroom, grateful that the disaster hadn't been worse, then got into the elevator with Partho, who continued snickering, even after Axel threw a hateful scowl in his direction.

"Geez, Axel . . . Aren't you embarrassed?" Partho asked, as compassionately as possible under the circumstances.

Axel met the boy's gaze. "Are *you* embarrassed?"

"Hell, yeah! I'm totally scandalized!"

"Okay," Axel shrugged. "You can be scandalized for both of us."

"What do you mean?" Partho pressed, though Axel clearly wanted him to forget the whole thing.

"I have cancer, Parth, and I just shit myself. Or rather, I just shit myself *again*. If I have to feel humiliated too, it will kill me. Do you understand? *It will fucking kill me.*" The red rings encircling Axel's eyes spoke volumes, so Partho dropped it.

Partho put his arm around his friend, who leaned into him, and defiantly refused to shed tears.

The tiny, cramped office of Milo Elliott might have been warm and inviting if it weren't so completely cluttered. Though he was uneasy in the crowded space, Axel thought the office suitably reflected the wiry and bookish Dr. Elliott, who sported the wild, unkempt facial hair of a man well beyond his 38 years. He explained that he was a hypnotherapist and asked that they call him by his first name, then suggested that he might be able to help ease the pain of treatment and perhaps assist with meditation techniques that might improve Axel's mental state. He asked a number of pointed questions about Axel's pain management and medications and took notes from Axel's jumbled, halting answers.

When it was Axel's turn to speak, he glanced at Partho as if the most articulate, desirable words were to be found on the boy's face. "I don't care about the pain. I mean, it's real, but I understand where it comes from, and I'm enduring it well enough. I'm exhausted on a cellular level just about all the time too, but that's okay, I think, at least for now." Axel licked his lips as Milo got him a cup of water from a dispenser nestled into the piles of files next to his desk. "I'm not sleeping very well, which isn't new or unusual, I guess. But I'm having these dreams . . ."

"What kind of dreams?" Milo asked, without granting the query the sense of importance Axel would have liked.

"Sharp, vibrant dreams. Which is strange, because my real, wide-awake world feels so muted and kind of detached right now."

"Do these dreams feel intuitive in any way? Like premonitions?"

Axel considered the possibility, but rejected it. "No. I don't really believe in that stuff. I mean, I've never even felt déjà vu or anything, though I think I understand what it must feel like to others. These dreams play out like memories that belong to somebody else." Axel speculated briefly about whether he sounded as stupid to others as he did to himself. "Like I've hijacked dreams that aren't really mine."

"Are you on any medication right now? Pain medication?"

Axel knew he was sending the wrong signals, but he didn't know how to get the untidy hypnotist to see that the issue wasn't related to medication or why the dreams seemed so important. "I have OxyContin with me, but I didn't want to be impaired when I got here."

Milo shrugged. "It actually might help with our process. Can I see?" Axel handed over his prescription bottle, and Milo squinted at the label. "How many do you usually take?"

"Just one. But I'm allowed two every six hours."

"Take two."

"What for?" Axel mumbled, though he was already swallowing the pills, grateful to have a specific medical command requiring him to do so.

"I want you to relax. In a few minutes, I'm going to put you under. If we're fortunate, maybe something useful will emerge." Milo turned to Partho. "Would you mind waiting outside?"

"Why can't I watch?" Partho whined with the intensity of a schoolboy about to be expelled from a dirty movie.

"No," Axel said firmly.

"I just watched you take a dump! You won't let me see you get hypnotized?"

Milo was already pushing his way toward the door, which he opened for Partho. "There's a coffee shop downstairs where you might be more comfortable."

Partho flipped Axel the bird as he left. "Fuck you, Axel." But Axel just waved goodbye as he waited for his OxyContin fog to deepen.

Milo told him he would be recording the session, asked if he had any questions, and then cleared out a space on the sofa for Axel to lie down.

"What if I fall asleep?"

"That might not be a bad thing, Axel. Just relax and listen to my voice. Let's try to free up your mind and see where it takes us. Picture someplace you like to be. Someplace where you feel warm and safe and happy. Go there now. Take deep breaths and as you exhale, release all the pain and tension and worry . . ."

Axel followed instructions and tried to release the rigging that moored his thoughts. He certainly didn't believe for a moment that he could be hypnotized. Not successfully, at least. But Milo's voice was soft and gentle, and he needed to surrender to something if he was ever going to figure anything out.

The OxyContin was making his head feel fantastically soft and airy, and he imagined puffy white clouds surrounding him and wafting in and out with his breath. Milo's voice sounded gentle and comforting and far away . . .

℘ ℘ ℘

"So how do you feel?" Milo asked, somewhat abruptly, and in a normal tone of voice. Axel opened his eyes and gazed around the cluttered office. The eye-goo matting his eyelids was a leading indicator that he had been out a while.

"I'm okay. I guess it didn't work." He looked at Milo for confirmation, but received no response. "Sorry for falling asleep."

"No apology necessary," Milo muttered as he reviewed the notes on the pad before him.

"What happened?" Axel was still feeling mellow and didn't wish to be so direct, but he wasn't being given much to work with.

Milo shrugged and made a few more notes as Axel began to feel ignored. Had the hypnotherapist just watched him snooze on his sofa or what? Axel squinted at Milo Elliott and blurted out the first thing that came into his head. "You haven't shaved since Priscilla left."

The lead in Milo Elliott's pencil snapped, and he looked up from the page with alarm in his eyes that fell just short of fear. The last person who had looked at Axel that way was Tommy, and the sharp sting he felt deep inside was almost too much to bear. "I'm sorry. I shouldn't have said anything."

Milo quietly slid his pad onto his desk and focused his attention entirely on Axel. "You sure you're feeling alright?"

Axel nodded slowly and wondered who the fuck Priscilla was. Milo reached over and pulled Axel's eyelid up as if he could more easily read his gray matter that way. Milo leaned back in his chair again, looking very professorial and concerned. After a moment, he spoke. "I'd like you to speak with one of my colleagues. She's not a colleague, really, she's more of a . . ." Axel could tell Milo was searching for a polite word for "crackpot." Moreover, he sensed that Milo believed she was the only person who might be able to help him. "Tell you what; I'll set up a meeting. Alright?"

Milo led Axel toward the door before he had a chance to object, and the next thing he knew, he was standing out in the hall with Partho.

"How did it go?"

"I fell asleep."

"Oh," Partho said, sounding disappointed.

They proceeded down the hall, then Axel abruptly turned and hurried back to knock on the office door. After a moment, it opened a crack. Axel stood silently for a moment, as if reconsidering, but then spoke as if he couldn't control himself. "I know how much you miss her, but she really wasn't the one," he said quietly. "The right one is on her way, but you have to shave or she's never going to recognize you."

Partho heard a mournful "thank you" from behind the door and then watched it close. Axel pushed his way past him to get to the elevator.

Partho didn't say anything for a while until he was sure Axel was fully awake and clear of whatever had happened in the office. Axel looked so frail and tired slumped against the passenger door, Partho had trouble believing this was the mountain biker whose skill he had once envied. Axel's head lolled toward Partho as if he understood. "When I get better, we're going to tackle the trails, and I am gonna kick the shit out of your sorry Hindu ass."

They rode in silence for a while longer before Partho started with the interrogation. "So who was the chick?"

"What chick?"

"Dude, I totally listened at the door. Who was the chick?" Axel couldn't help but smile. Southern California colloquialisms like *chick* and *dude* still sounded hilarious when filtered through Parth's ever so slight Mumbai accent.

"There was no chick."

Partho couldn't tell if Axel was pulling his leg. He had gone downstairs to the café, but was only gone a few minutes. "I heard her voice. There was somebody in there. A girl," he insisted.

Axel shrugged, as if it all happened too long ago to be important. "I was asleep, and his office was kinda messy. Maybe he had a hooker under his desk?"

"I don't give a fuck if you tell me what happened or not," Partho said, which indicated he very much *did* give a fuck. "You should have seen yourself taking a crap. Scandalous!"

ᗅ   ᗅ   ᗅ

Milo Elliott sat alone in his office that night, trying to keep an open mind. He had always strived to achieve a good balance between the completely rational and the doubtful but possible. He was not easily shaken, but his hands trembled as he reached across his desk and once again backed up his digital recorder. He hesitated before pressing the button that would replay his session with Axel Hooley. In other circumstances, he might convince himself that Axel was a phony, but there was no shred of evidence that the sick, guileless man on his sofa only hours before was capable of such deception. He would no doubt listen to the recording over and over into the night: and probably wouldn't sleep any better than his patient, at least not for a good long while.

He pressed the Play button on his recorder, and a strong, self-assured, vaguely accented ephemeral voice issued from the machine. *"I am called Balanos, daughter of Oxylus and Hamadryas. Bound for life to the sturdiest Oak in Carnalbanagh in the Contae Aontroma near Slemish Mountain."*

Milo quickly turned the machine off, as if some force from beyond might punch a hole into his grimy office and drag him off. "Holy shit," he muttered under his breath. "Holy fucking shit."

# Chapter 15

## Surfing the Treetops

Axel joked that it took Dale less than six months to transform Tommy into a gay pastiche of June Cleaver, Carol Brady, Clare Huxtable, and Marge Simpson. The union of Tommy and Dale vastly improved the circumstances of both parties, which is how Axel figured things were supposed to work, but only rarely ever did. Domestic bliss had also come with an additional 15 pounds, which Tommy's frame could handle certainly, but it robbed him of the trendy, starved look so popular on the coasts.

Tommy worked a few hours a week for a location scout, but his burning desire to set the film industry on its ear had been slaked to a large extent by conjugal harmony. He showed a knack for cooking and a flair for decorating; neither of which had been displayed, exercised, or remotely practiced in any manner whatsoever during all the years he shared an apartment with Axel.

Tommy scoured the internet seeking exotic destinations and planning elaborate vacations, which he and Dale thoroughly enjoyed. After some cost-conscious negotiating with the more sensible and money-minded of the two, they began alternating their big trips with smaller, inexpensive weekend getaways. Brussels was thus followed by a weekend on Catalina Island, the romance of Tuscany preceded a sweltering junket to Palm Springs, and so on. Sometimes Axel was included in what came to be known as the "cheap trips."

The hiking excursion to Zion National Park in Utah was Dale's suggestion initially, as he had gone camping there with the Junior Mounties or the Fuzzy Beavers, or whatever scouting organization was in vogue during his idyllic Canadian youth. Zion was more elaborate than their usual weekend getaways, but far less excessive than their big trips. Tommy was always meticulous with Dale's schedule and conscious of his need to be in email contact, but the arrest of one of Dale's investment clients on federal charges threw a monkey wrench into their best laid plans. Dale insisted that Tommy take Axel on the trip rather than cancel and pledged to join them as soon as he helped clear his client of insider trading charges.

Axel immediately began thinking of the trip to Zion as the swan song for their ongoing day-to-day friendship. Tommy and Dale were becoming the sort of couple who socialized more and more with other couples, and Axel's presence wasn't adding anything of real value to the mix. He could never walk away from his friends, of course, but felt that the prudent thing to do was to back slowly toward the outskirts of their social circle. Dale and Tommy fancied themselves the most perfect unit since the atom, and Axel wanted to get out of the way before he triggered some sort of unpleasant nuclear reaction.

If this was going to be their last escapade, Axel wanted to do whatever he could to make it memorable. Something unique to Tommy and him. Something exciting that he would never be able to carry off with anybody else. The answer was so obvious that it might as well have been lit up with bright chaser lights – *hang gliders!* He doubted that they were legal for use on federal land, but it was always easier to ask forgiveness than permission, and ignorance had always been a powerful tool as far as Axel was concerned. Besides, all those mountains and ledges were just aching to be leapt from. And there would probably be a lot of fir trees around if anybody needed to cushion their fall.

They spent their first three days scouting their preferred takeoff locations before settling on Angel's Landing. Horse Ranch Mountain was the highest peak in Zion, but Angel's Landing was nearer the center of the park, and Axel felt that the smooth, slanted rock would give them a better running start. And there were stunning views in every direction, which might provide options, depending on how the wind was behaving.

Angel's Landing was also one of the most spectacular hikes imaginable, featuring a narrow ridge with deep chasms plunging 1,400 feet or so on either side. Part of the trail included chains jutting out of the sandy mountains, designed to assist hikers with the rugged climb.

Axel and Tommy sat in their tent at night and crafted their plan in eerie silhouette thrown by the flame from their Coleman lantern. Their cumbersome hang gliding equipment would have to be spirited up the hill in three separate trips to conceal the aluminum pieces in the underbrush until they could retrieve them for launch. Their third and final hike would take place in the early morning and was to culminate in a quick assembly and subsequent takeoff from the lofty plateau.

Their first two hikes came off without a hitch, and they found some scrubby brush in which to conceal their equipment without much difficulty. Their third hike up the mountain began in the cold morning hours when *Refrigerator Canyon* very much lived up to its name. Axel's favorite part of the hike was a segment called "Walter's Wiggles," a series of 21 switchbacks, which carried them from the canyon floor up the side of the mountain in an efficient and exhilarating manner. In their disassembled form, their rented hang gliders could be mistaken for an elaborate tent if they were spotted by park rangers or fellow hikers.

Their intent was to hike to the top and unload the equipment, and then backtrack briefly to retrieve the parts they had stashed in the underbrush. The only other hikers they saw or spoke with that morning were a cheerful Norwegian couple with enough familiarity with the English language to successfully navigate themselves through a hike in a remote area, but little else. They grinned cautiously from their perch atop the landing as they watched Axel and Tommy scurry off the plateau for 15 minutes or so to retrieve their additional equipment. And they didn't bother them during most of the assembly process, which took longer than Axel thought it should have, particularly the meticulous stretching of the nylon fabric over the aluminum frames.

It wasn't until it became glaringly obvious what they were doing did the cheery Norwegians turn somber and approach. The man spoke in a cajoling, though vaguely threatening manner, so Axel just smiled and nodded and pointed off into the distance and waved at an imaginary comrade in order to distract them.

"What do you think, Axel?" The waver in Tommy's voice was a clear indication that he was getting cold feet.

The four of them stood blinking at each other for a moment before the large man began hurtling himself back down the trail, waving his arms and shouting an alarm that Axel didn't need a phrasebook to interpret.

God damn these meddling foreigners, Axel thought, simultaneously reprimanding himself for not being more open-minded with regard to the convictions of hearty strangers concerning personal welfare, responsibility, and park rules. It seemed unreasonable that they should go to all the trouble of making travel plans, flying across the ocean, and enduring American customs procedures in order to belligerently tattle on them.

"Maybe we shouldn't try it," Tommy said softly.

Axel flashed suddenly on Rachel's office at the University – a framed sampler on her bookshelf quoted Pearl S. Buck in fading, homey embroidery: *"Every great mistake has a halfway moment, a split second when it can be recalled and perhaps remedied."* It seemed meaningless at the time, but Axel soon understood that he had missed his golden Pearl S. Buck moment. For years afterward, he imagined he might possess a time machine enabling him to go back and choose differently.

"You can carry your shit down the mountain if you want to, buttface, but I'm gonna fly!"

In one daring and reckless move, Axel sprinted toward the southwest edge and pushed off from the rock. He arced his delta wing and sailed gracefully toward a peak called The Spearhead, then shifted his weight toward the left to catch a thermal lift and climb into the open air. The next thing he knew, he was soaring blissfully over the canyon, but couldn't see Tommy either to his left or to his right. He looped toward the river at his first opportunity in order to catch a glimpse back at Angel's Landing. He could see Tommy struggling with the Amazonian Norwegian woman who held tightly to his nose wires and control bar. She seemed to have the upper hand, though Tommy was firmly strapped into his glider. If he could just manage to scare the gargantuan woman away for a moment, Tommy might be able to get a running start. The wind took Axel again and he quickly realized that he'd better pay some attention to his own plight before he became too concerned with Tommy.

Axel rode the air currents, trying to maintain control and had the good fortune to catch an updraft, which propelled him higher. He shifted his weight forcefully and arced back toward Angel's Landing despite the risk of slamming into the side of the mountain. He had to do something bold, or Tommy wasn't even going to get off the ground. He wobbled slightly, as he soared toward Amazonia, still comfortably riding the crest of his updraft. He lifted as he drew near and managed to kick the side of her head and knock her to the ground. It wasn't his most proudly chivalrous moment, but he had to hold onto the control bar with both hands and he was running perilously short on options. He glimpsed Tommy running toward the west on the plateau as Axel skimmed off toward the east.

Axel's newly hatched fledgling was off and soaring on his own, or at least that's what he imagined. Thanks to the intrusive Norwegians, the peak of Angel's landing now jutted majestically between them. There wasn't anything Axel could do about it now anyway, as the air currents on the eastern side of the peak had a schema of their own and he knew better than to ask any more of the wind than had already generously been delivered.

He soared over Valley Road, and then east toward Hidden Canyon. They had scouted several potential landing sites, but would now probably come down in two different locations altogether.

It felt glorious and magical. Soaring above the treetops was the most natural thing Axel could imagine. It was more instinctive than walking or skiing, or even breathing. He connected with something raw and primal and felt more innately himself than ever before. He would have been content flying forever, and surfed gracefully over the tops of a few dozen evergreens before he lost the wind and was forced to ditch his LiteSport in their boughs, release his harness, and drop to the ground. The rented hang glider was shredded, but it was totally worth it, he thought as he made his way back to the main road.

Axel never found out if Tommy got to enjoy any of the flight before he crashed into Cathedral Mountain and fell to his death. In retrospect, it seemed almost impossible that the whole thing had ever been a good idea, and there was nobody to blame but himself for instigating and then pursuing the harebrained plan with such fervor.

Axel wanted Dale to beat the holy shit out of him because he plainly deserved it, and was crushed when Dale handled everything with predictable heartbreak, gentleness, and solemnity. Dale did manage to ask him what the fuck they thought they were doing, but Axel could only shake his head and surrender to a state of near-catatonic despair. When Zoë arrived later that night, she held Axel for a long time while his body was racked with sobs. When he calmed down, she whispered quietly into his ear, "Gravity is a harsh mistress," which, surprisingly enough, kind of helped.

Axel thought about leaving the coast after Tommy died, mostly out of shame. It all seemed so unbelievable and more like a dream after a while – a feeling Axel welcomed because it was easier than the ugly reality. How could he have failed to think things through a little better?

In the end, he decided to stay in Los Angeles because he realized that no matter how far he ran, he was never going to outrun losing Tommy.

# Chapter 16

## Into The Weeds

Despite the numerous offers of assistance and the stalwart reliability of everyone else, Partho had become Axel's most constant driver. The wisdom of Partho's inclusion on the Death Watch List was so frequently apparent that Axel's initial reluctance to include him seemed plain silly. Partho made the most of his new-found opportunity to talk about his dead mother – something he had apparently never done up until now. During the many hours they had spent hiking and biking together, Axel and Partho hadn't, in fact, managed much conversation, but chatter flowed naturally and constantly now that they were mostly sitting and waiting. Axel had begun experiencing quiet phases where his mind seemed to shut down, but Partho's young, first-generation alien take on things kept him engaged in ways that none of his other friends were able to mimic. Besides, Partho could not truly be offended, and God knows Axel worked overtime trying.

Axel avoided thinking about the additional pressure he felt resulting from their blossoming friendship – the amplified obligation to survive was too great a burden to dwell on. Failing himself or his other friends was one thing, but failing a sweet-faced kid who had been so tragically let down in the past would be unforgivable.

They were unusually quiet on their way to Axel's fourth round of chemotherapy, probably because they both had a good idea what to expect – three days of steady, but not life-threatening, decline, followed by an abrupt body slam into the wall on day four. The subsequent desperate hours might include hospitalization, possibly more neutropenia, and no doubt some discussion about removing his chemotherapy early, which would cheat him out of the full dose. If all went well, however, the infusion unit would inject the last of its poison through his PICC line into his cephalic vein on day five, and the empty chemotherapy infusion unit would then be removed.

A dozen days of physical hell would follow, including another dose or two of Neulasta, and would most definitely be accompanied by greater physical pain and discomfort. Each round of chemotherapy was progressively more grueling, but if he got through this one, there was only one last cycle scheduled. Since round three, Partho had generally approached the whole process with more solemnity than Axel was comfortable with and certainly far more reverence than he wanted, but he found himself in no condition to put forth the effort to lighten the mood.

A dozen patients of varying ages and stages of decay were scattered about the infusion room, all having at least two starkly contrasting things in common – cancer, of course, and the equally obvious good fortune to be treated for it in Beverly Hills.

There were two types of chemotherapy on Axel's menu for today. Partho watched with fascination while one of their favorite nurses, Freida, prepared the large injection tube with the dark, ominous liquid for the *push*. The *push* was so named because Freida would push the plunger slowly and inject the contents of the syringe into Axel's PICC line over the course of ten or fifteen minutes. Freida had been an oncology nurse for thirty years, loved the patients, knew when and how to talk to them, and what to say when she did. She also understood when quiet hand-holding worked best.

"It looks like purple Kool-Aid," Partho offered, somewhat awkwardly when they were about to begin the process.

"Yeah," Axel sighed. "*Toxic* Kool-Aid."

"This won't be so bad. The 5-FU infusion is the real bitch." Frieda often directed her explanations to the patient's companion, which Axel thought was nice. Frieda made it feel like she and the patient were insiders who somehow *understood.* Spouses, family members, and friends were the real neophytes that she was helping along. Frieda settled into a chair opposite Axel and began the procedure.

"My mother died of cancer," Partho chimed in after a moment. Axel caught Frieda's eye and shrugged almost imperceptibly.

Frieda was unruffled. "I'm sorry to hear that. What kind?"

"Breast, then everywhere else I suppose."

"So your mother had chemotherapy?"

"I think she did. It was long ago – forever, really. I was very young."

Frieda's eyes again passed Axel's and they shared a bemused moment. Axel could recall when his own forever had only stretched to 16 years.

"I don't remember her very well."

"She'd be pleased to see you've grown into such a fine young man," Frieda said. "You always take such good care of your father."

Axel thought she was joking at first, and then was offended once he realized that Frieda actually believed he and Partho were father and son. Despite the biological possibility, considering the difference in their respective ages, Axel considered himself far too young to have fathered a boy of 16. Partho, on the other hand, found the idea sidesplittingly funny.

"We aren't even the same race," Axel insisted, still hoping he'd misunderstood.

Frieda stayed focused on the slow movement of the plunger into the syringe, but glanced up at Axel for another look. "Really? You're a tough one in that regard. You could be just about anything."

"Don't be fooled. He's really my creepy uncle who's usually kept in the attic," Partho snorted.

Axel wished they'd both just shut the hell up so he could focus on the noxious intravenous Kool-Aid's slow progression into his arteries. The last thing he wanted to be reminded of was that his own heritage continued to be in question.

"The two of you have such rapport, I just assumed you were related."

"This is L.A.," Axel shrugged at Partho. "It's all the rage to have a trendy ethnic baby flown in from Calcutta for adoption."

"Bite me, Uncle Pervy." Partho giggled. Axel laughed a little, too, sincerely hoping that it would help.

The push was followed half an hour later with the connection of the 5-FU chemotherapy infusion unit. Two hours of observation were required to insure that everything was working as designed and that Axel wasn't having any immediate ill-effects. This was precautionary, however, because by this time everyone involved anticipated, with good reason, that Axel's particular brand of ill effects would wait until day four to tap dance onto the scene.

Axel checked the time on Partho's Rolex as they waited for the valet to bring the Porsche around. One nice thing about the Oncologist's office was they always validated parking, which was rare for medical offices in Beverly Hills, where people were accustomed to paying for valet parking, even at the post office. They were efficient, too, as the whole process from arrival to departure took less than three hours. Dr. Kenn and his staff did everything possible to make the necessarily shitty lives of cancer patients hassle free.

It was spitting rain outside, so Partho took a moment to put the roof up on the car. He called to Axel within earshot and for the benefit of the car hiker. "Try not to shit on the upholstery, Daddy."

"Stop calling me that, you insipid little fuck."

"It's a compliment. It would be great if you were my dad."

"Great for *who?*"

"Great for all of us. My Dad's an asshole."

Axel hoped that Partho's father spent more time with the boy than Isaac Hooley had ever bothered whiling away with him, though he sincerely doubted that the professional demands on Mr. Mishra's time afforded him that luxury.

It felt unfair for Axel to think poorly of the Hooleys, as they had done the best they could, given their limited world view. Besides, the McKennas had ultimately been more than generous with their time and affection, even if they did come to the party late and were called away early. If indeed that's the role Axel was meant to fulfill for Partho, he thought perhaps he should start putting forth a little more effort? Could that be who he was supposed to be? A substitute father who was there by accident, or just because he decided, for whatever reason, to give a damn? What would Tad McKenna say to Partho right now? Something pithy and wise and effortless, no doubt.

"Parth," he said, with a sharper tone than he intended, as they wheeled out onto Doheny. "I can't even look after myself."

"You don't have to, Daddy-O. That's why I'm here."

Axel resisted the impulses tugging on his emotions. He tried not to cry for himself, though he'd recently begun weeping openly and at length at Hallmark commercials. Partho was maturing into a terrific human being, despite the Porsche and the Rolex and the hideous Gucci sandals. By contrast, there wasn't a single thing Axel could offer him that hadn't already been provided or that he wouldn't eventually stumble into on his own. Axel could never become any sort of Tad McKenna, for Partho or anybody else. He was just a diseased indigent who needed a ride.

"I couldn't be left in charge of Tommy for a whole weekend without killing him. I am not a responsible soul, nor will I likely ever be, so please quit insinuating that I am."

"Sorry," Partho said, sounding sincerely regretful. "I forgot about that time you killed your friend."

"And I would never be able to afford to give you a sports car or a $1,000 wristwatch, either. I'm absolutely certain that you are the apple of your father's eye, whether he tucks you in at night or not."

"My watch retails for nearly $4,500, Axel—"

"You remind him of his dead wife who he loved more than anything, and as delightful as that sounds, most of the time it's gotta be pretty fucking awful!" Axel was even more shocked by his outburst than Partho, and immediately wanted to suck the words back.

Partho glanced at Axel, uneasily. "They say I look like her, but how—?"

"I don't know how, okay?! I don't *know* anything." Axel stared out the window at the rapidly escalating rain. "Just fucking drive."

"Yas'm, Miz Daisy."

Axel made it another two blocks before he cracked a smile, and Partho caught him because he was watching for it. "You're a fucking prick, Partho. My dead best friend, cancer, and questionable racial slurs inspired by award-winning cinema, are not appropriate grist for your adolescent comedy mill."

Partho chuckled triumphantly. "Yes, I know. You've been a terrible influence, Papa."

The copious steps up the hill to Dale's house were exhausting under normal circumstances and downright insurmountable in the pouring rain. They sat in the car for five long minutes before Partho broke the silence. "Do you think you're ready?"

Axel shrugged and nodded and opened his door as Partho scurried around the car to help. Axel wondered aloud whether there were nerve endings in bone marrow because all the shots of Neulasta were making his skeleton ache. The railing alongside the steps was rickety – simple PVC pipe that was perfectly practical most of the time, but insufficient in torrential rainstorms. Axel cursed himself for wearing flip flops instead of going to the extra trouble of socks and sneakers. Such mundane luxuries as warm, dry, rubber-soled shoes seemed to take impossible amounts of time and energy to achieve.

Axel made a half-assed attempt at a running start and cleared a total of eight steps before he had to stop to gasp for air. Partho ducked in beneath his arm and braced him around the waist.

They took another dozen steps before Axel halted again and rolled his head toward his friend. "You're getting wet."

"Who gives a flying fuck, Axel?"

Axel grimaced. He'd had the salty tongue of a sailor ever since college, but he didn't like to see that element of himself rubbing off on Partho. "I can do this. Why don't you go back to the car."

"Just keep moving and stop being a jerk."

Another five or six steps. Rest. Two more. Longer rest. Then five. He felt leaden and brittle and more than a tad dizzy.

"Careful, Parth. I don't want to drag you down with me."

"Too late for that, Uncle Pervy," Parth said with a chuckle that was apparently contagious because Axel started laughing and lost his balance. He released his grip on Partho's shoulder and grasped the flimsy railing for support, which wobbled and then shifted abruptly in the muck. Partho lunged and caught Axel's sweatshirt, overcompensating for the lack of ballast by jerking him upright too quickly. They teetered for a hopeful moment as Axel's feet groped for purchase on a slippery step, then they tumbled off the side altogether.

It was then that the soggy pair fell victim to what Dale referred to as the *hillside conundrum*. Local regulations dictated that hillsides be kept clear of brush and debris in order to impede brush fires – and the subsequent lack of vegetation on those same hills thus facilitated mudslides. The hillside conundrum was, to some extent, unavoidable, though few victims of the dilemma had ever been caught quite so utterly unprepared, or so completely fallen prey to their circumstances.

All 40 of their fingers and toes grappled in vain for the weeds and vines that flourished in abundance on California slopes everywhere. The foliage on their particular hillside, unfortunately, had that day surrendered to the shears and weed whackers of Dale's ever diligent biweekly gardening crew. The skid down the hill was a particular thrill for Partho, who had never been on a ski slope. They came to stop in a muddy pile at the bottom, next to the Porsche, with Axel cursing a blue streak, which didn't stop until Partho clapped a hand over his mouth.

"Tell me again, Axel."

"Tell you what?" Axel muttered, his voice muffled by Partho's palm.

"Tell me how this isn't anything to joke about."

Twenty minutes later, Axel crawled up onto Dale's front portico with Partho, providing an occasional shove from behind for encouragement. "I wonder if Dale is actually planning to grow old on this stupid motherfucking hill?"

Sylvia and Esperanza were lounging on the front portico, crowded onto one chaise, each blowing gently into their respective bubble wands. Synthetic soap bubbles wafted gently toward Axel, and then drifted beyond the safety of the overhang where they abruptly popped in the rain. Axel didn't wish to appear needy, but was put off by their lack of concern for his recent, apparent, and horrendous plight. He figured that if he sprawled there long enough, they'd come around.

"You're getting *awfully* handsome," Sylvia purred between bubbles.

"Thanks," Axel responded, unsure exactly what to make of the compliment, given his mud encrusted condition and the fact that he had lost 45 pounds and was practically unconscious.

"I'm not talking about *you,* darling. You look like . . . what is it? 'Death on a cracker.' That's it — you look like death on a cracker!" Sylvia jerked her head toward Partho, who had plopped onto the porch and was scraping the mud off his sandals with a stick. "I'm talking about your little buddy. He's really getting quite nice."

"Thank you, ma'am," Partho nodded politely. Axel didn't know if Partho could tell that the sultry old broad was flirting with him.

"There's so much rain this year," Sylvia sighed. "Do you think we're having an *El Camino?*"

"You mean *El Niño,*" Esperanza corrected. "El Camino is a butt-ugly car."

"Oh?" Sylvia looked perplexed. "I thought it was a butt-ugly truck."

"It's both," Axel said, as he summoned the strength to drag himself to his feet. "This isn't an El Niño, Sylvia. It's just rain."

Something wasn't quite right, but Axel couldn't put his finger on it. Sylvia and Esperanza serenely sharing a chaise was just wrong, wrong, wrong, and the two of them inhabiting the same mellow, nonconfrontational atmosphere felt inappropriate to the point of being bone-chilling. Axel festered in place for another moment until it was apparent that assistance wasn't forthcoming, and then finished pulling himself upright and staggered in through the front door.

Zoë was stretched out on the sofa looking sleepy while Damien gave her a foot rub. Damien looked up, slightly dazed, and gave Axel a silly grin. "Hey, Axel. I'm on a layover, so I came by to take care of you."

"Uh, thanks," Axel said, feeling very much in need of the tender loving care that was obviously being squandered on others. "How's Vegas?" he asked, and wondered why Damien hadn't complimented him on how good he looked. Everyone saw Axel deteriorating, and the mud didn't help his look any, but he'd grown accustomed to new arrivals complimenting him on his appearance ever since he'd begun looking like an actual cadaver. If any praise were forthcoming, they'd better get to it quick before Partho followed him inside and once again stole his thunder. Instead of answering the question, Damien just looked confused. Axel sighed. "So where's Dale?"

"Oh, that's right," Zoë sat upright and tried to focus. "Dale went to Winnipeg."

Axel was stunned at the blatant and seemingly universal lack of concern. How could Dale have gone on a trip when he so clearly needed him? He was days away from his entire vulnerable system raising holy hell, and nobody gave a shit. "How could he—? What the f—? I can't *believe* he went on goddamn holiday—!" Axel continued to sputter as the mud flaked off his sweatpants onto the floor.

Zoë let him go until he spun himself out, then proceeded methodically. "His father had a heart attack, Axel."

"Oh . . . So he went to *Vancouver?*"

Zoë clouded over with confusion. "Is that where Dale's from? Vancouver?"

Axel nodded.

"Oh. Then that's where he went — Vancouver. I wonder where I got 'Winnipeg?'"

Axel couldn't even enjoy a decent tantrum without having the wind knocked out of his sails. "So . . . a heart attack, huh? Is it bad?"

"Yes, Axel," Zoë nodded, as if patiently turning on the light in the bedroom of a dim-witted child. "Heart attacks are *bad.*" She lay back and again stuck her feet into Damien's lap, where he resumed the massage without the slightest hint of sexual arousal, which was no big surprise. "Oh, and he didn't have time to shop, so we're out of food."

"Well I don't know what you expect me to do about it," Axel snapped. He was gunning for a fight, but couldn't seem to drum up any interest. In the absence of their host, Axel figured most of these people would starve to death.

"We're okay. Your friend Cheryl dropped off some brownies, and oh my God were they yummy!"

Baked goods from Cheryl — with the emphasis on *baked.* That certainly explained things. His friends were bonding as a result of his illness, but not to the point where everybody knew exactly the sorts of specific things everybody else was up to. It hadn't occurred to Axel, in his constant state of nausea, that the general populace might be seduced by sweet treats. He considered enlightening Zoë, but decided to keep it to himself. If she knew how much pot she'd ingested, she might give him more of a squabble than he was really up for. Besides, an urgent trip to the market would be inevitable once everybody got the munchies.

Axel didn't want to track mud through the house, so he shimmied out of his sweats and T-shirt, then tottered into the kitchen in his underpants to get a drink. Dignity had been abandoned long before the sweatpants, and the citizens of *Chez Cancer* were accustomed to seeing the wreckage of his body parading past in various stages of undress.

Despite the lack of groceries, Rhymey was toiling over several pots and pans simmering away on the stove. Axel figured Rhymey could probably raise a hearty meal from sawdust and toenail clippings if it came to that. Without saying a word, Rhymey hurried to the refrigerator and took out an Ensure and a vitamin water. He handed both to Axel with a grin and a clap on the shoulder that seemed simultaneously friendly and invasive. "I washed some warm quilts for your little bed."

Axel nodded and returned to the living room. Partho had come inside, looking comparatively mud free, all things considered. Axel gazed at Zoë and Damien. "I'm sorry to hear about Dale's dad. I hope he's going to be alright."

Zoë shrugged and opened her eyes slightly. "Sometimes family just takes priority, Axel."

"No shit," Axel said as he headed toward the luxurious tub in Dale's upstairs bathroom.

"Do you need help?" Partho asked conscientiously, having clearly missed out on the brownies.

"No, thanks, Parth," Axel said, raising his hand in a lackluster wave. Good old, reliable, sober Partho. Partho was at least as grown-up as his other friends. In fact, everybody Axel had surrounded himself with seemed to have about the exact same level of maturity. "I draw the line somewhere short of getting a sponge bath from a teenage boy."

"I don't!" Damien looked up optimistically, suddenly quite alert.

"Keep your hands off the jail bait, you randy gaymo," Axel sighed. As he plodded upstairs, he guessed that might be the last millisecond of levity he'd get for a long while. He paused on the landing to rest, then continued upward, filthy, disheartened and sicker every moment.

# Chapter 17

## Linnea Fanshaw

Milo Elliot had already commandeered a table at Cafe Talésai on the Sunset Strip shortly before noon when Axel arrived. Axel didn't recognize him immediately because he was clean shaven and easily looked a whole decade younger. He motioned for Axel to sit down as he mumbled goodbyes into his phone, nodding as if the caller could observe and appreciate his firm grasp of their exchange.

Their meeting was supposed to have taken place the day before, but Milo cancelled because of a scheduling conflict with the woman he wanted Axel to meet. All Axel was told was that she was clairvoyant or an intuitive or something ridiculous, yet compelling enough that he was obliged to drag himself to West Hollywood on day four of his 5-FU chemotherapy infusion. He might have felt edgy and nervous if the chemo hadn't completely dulled his ability to feel anything but despair.

Maude had dropped him off and promised to return in just over an hour to gather him up and take him back to Dale's in Silverlake. Aside from Maude, who was a portrait of discretion, he hadn't told anyone about the meeting and he hadn't asked Partho to drive because Partho could be difficult to shake. Besides, his telephone conversation with Milo had been so convoluted and preposterous, he felt that pursuing this alone was the prudent thing to do. Everyone on the Death Watch List was near the phone, poised to swoop in if he needed them, and Milo could drive him to the emergency room if he experienced an immediate crisis.

Axel had grown to despise going out in public, particularly in Beverly Hills or West Hollywood, where the locals were not particularly forgiving with regard to a lack of physical attractiveness, and at this point there certainly wasn't any way he could skate by on charm. At least Cafe Talésai would inevitably burgeon into a franchised corporate Thai conglomerate and therefore didn't count as real restaurant in Axel's book.

Milo had scarcely greeted Axel when the reason for their meeting swept into the room. Axel hoped that was who it was anyway because she had the stunning looks and bearing of someone you really wanted to be seen sharing a table with, even at Cafe Talésai. She spotted them immediately and sailed past the hostess, flashing a smile that would have put a charging rhino at ease. She strode straight toward Axel with laser-like focus that was more mesmerizing than alarming and stood for a moment as if she were looking straight into him. "You must be Axel Hooley," she said, then flung her bag under the table, knelt gently in the booth next to him, and took his hand. "Of course, you are. Who else would you be? What an evil, horrible disease."

"Axel, this is Linnea Fanshaw," Milo said, with an odd sense of pride, as if he had invented her, or at the very least been credited for planting his flag on her terrain.

Linnea was a walking optical illusion – she looked tall, though she probably wasn't over five foot six. She seemed young, though the merry lines around her eyes and mouth indicated that she must certainly be well over fifty. She wore a short skirt, textured hose, heels, and a faux leather biker jacket that would have been cheap and age-inappropriate on anybody else, yet somehow managed to look stunning hanging off her manly, square shoulders. The shoulders, of course, only served to make the rest of her appear even more feminine. Red lips, spiky jet black hair, and blue-green eyes. It was her eyes that always struck people, Axel thought. Then he realized he hadn't *thought* it at all – he *knew* it, though he wasn't exactly sure how. Somebody should design contact lenses in that color and name them simply "Linnea." She looked like she should have tattoos, though none were evident.

Axel looked at Milo, who seemed to be reflecting the light spilling off Linnea. Axel understood this to be an odd analysis, even as he made it, but it was true – even squirrely little Milo was more handsome while Linnea was in range. "You said she was a nut."

Milo looked aghast, and Axel realized he was again failing to censor himself. "I didn't say she was a *nut*, Axel—"

Linnea just grinned and kept her focus steady on Axel as she spoke. "That's alright, Milo, you may have just thought it loudly enough for Axel to hear."

"You scare me, Axel." Milo shook his head and dived into his menu. "And I did an eight month internship working with the criminally insane."

She leaned in to Axel and feigned a whisper. "Don't let him upset you. I'm relatively harmless."

The waitress came for their drink order, but they went ahead and ordered food just to get it out of the way. Axel requested a green curry appetizer, which he figured he couldn't stomach, but not ordering anything seemed impolite because the server was a struggling single mother trying to get by on tips. Axel didn't know where such a wild assumption came from, so he flicked it aside. He could only process so much raw material, after all, and thoughts and ideas that should have been innocuous had begun hitting him with the force of a battering ram.

"Why the curry?" Linnea asked, though Axel felt she didn't really think it was important. The notion that she was merely trying to keep him plugged into the here and now crossed his mind.

"Because . . ." Axel wanted his response to be a thoughtful one. "Because it's all green and vile and churning. It will feel right at home inside me right now."

Linnea gave a laugh that was more of a honk. It was so abrupt and unladylike that it brought a smile to Axel's face. Linnea looked to Milo. "You're right, Milo – I like him. I like him a lot."

Axel kept checking the time as they made small talk, worried about how long he had before his ability to function and think clearly might become too appallingly compromised. Linnea seemed to sense this and stroked his arm gently to let him know she was getting to the point.

"Milo thinks I might be able to help you with your dreams."

"Look at me," Axel spoke quietly and shook his head. "I haven't got any fucking dreams."

"I mean the dreams you have when you're asleep, not your shattered hopes and expectations," Linnea said, almost embarrassed. Then she brightened, unexpectedly. "Although maybe I can help with those, too."

"Maybe the dreams are chemically induced?" Milo speculated. "They might go away when he finishes his chemo."

"Maybe," Linnea seemed to agree. "But I suspect that both the dreams and I are here for reasons above and beyond Axel's treatment for cancer."

"Not your cancer specifically," Milo clarified. "You're so thoroughly depleted right now, it affords Linnea some advantages she might not have if you get well."

Axel and Linnea both blinked at Milo. Axel spoke first. "You said *if*."

"I'm sorry," Milo fumbled. "*When* you get well. Of course you're going to get well."

Axel turned back to Linnea. "Okay, then – advantages. What kind of advantages?"

"Linnea thinks you might be a faerie," Milo interjected, this time with a broad grin and a twinkle in his eye.

If Axel's blood hadn't been flowing so sluggishly, he would have blushed. "Jesus Christ! I only did it that *one time,* and me and Tommy were both so drunk I don't even think that counts—" Axel halted mid-sentence and cocked his head. "How do you know about *that?*"

Now it was Linnea's turn to blush. "I don't, really. I mean, I'm good, but I'm not *that* good. By 'faerie,' I mean—"

"She thinks you're a sixteenth century European wood nymph," Milo interrupted gleefully, with what appeared to be skeptical satisfaction at having stated it so bluntly.

Linnea quickly lept in to clarify. "*Celtic* wood nymph. Definitely Celtic. And now that I see you in the flesh, you're probably seventeenth century, not sixteenth. I don't know what I was thinking. Now that we're face to face, it's perfectly clear."

"Wow," Axel stared. "For some reason that doesn't sound any better than *fairy*."

"A *'Hamadryad'*, more specifically. A hamadryad known historically as *Balanos*. One of the seven dryads borne of Greek mythology. All sisters." Linnea paused, but Axel didn't react. "You're quite famous, really, and very well documented, at least as far as dryads go."

Axel considered this for a stoic moment. "A famous . . . well documented . . . *wood nymph?* Nope – still not better than *fairy*."

"If it helps any, I don't buy it either," Milo offered, and then seemed to back down. "But there's certainly something going on that defies reason. If Linnea can't get to the bottom of it, nobody can."

"And 'mythical,' too?" Axel asked Linnea, doing his best to ignore Milo. "So I'm a myth?"

"Hamadryads spring from Greek mythology, as I said, or at least they did initially," Linnea explained, obviously trying to assemble a response that might package more appealingly. "But myths come from somewhere – often very real things. We just don't put as much stock in the intangible these days, and faith is in tragically short supply."

"Faith?" Axel queried, uncertain of exactly what he was asking. He felt like an idiot for not being able to process more quickly and for formulating only vague responses that weren't even real questions.

"The Bible is a myth, for example; it's just a more commonly accepted one. Eve didn't actually eat an apple, you know. If she existed at all, she fucked Adam's brains out long before it even occurred to her that an apple a day might toss paradise away. But you certainly can't shove something like *that* down people's throats without being stoned by the Baptists."

"And when you think about it," Milo added, as Linnea threw him another withering look. "Why would God hold back on something as great as sex? I mean, what else do we *get?*"

Now his head was reeling, but Linnea was managing to hold his attention, so Axel nodded in the hope that she would continue, perhaps in such a way that he could somehow make sense of it all.

"Spirits spring from any number of sources – some come from the angelic realm, or the nature realm, like you, for example. A lot of us – a whole lot of us come up through the animal kingdom, which is a particularly arduous route, I can tell you from first-hand experience—"

"Okay," Axel interrupted, hoping to move things along a bit more quickly. After all, his clock was ticking. "These wooden whatever-they-are—."

"*Wood nymphs,*" Linnea nodded. "Or tree spirits. They're in the same general classification as brownies and leprechauns, so you've no need to worry – it's not as if you're a banshee or a bean nighe or anything horrible."

"Thanks," Axel said, sounding more sarcastic than he'd intended.

"Wood nymphs are bound to a single tree for life – in your case, an oak. While the tree grows and thrives, the spirit, too, will grow and thrive. When the tree dies, by whatever means, the wood nymph dies too, or at least that's the commonly accepted theory."

"But they don't always die?" Axel asked, grateful to have formulated a lucid and useful question.

"Some do, I suppose. But some – and my guess is you might be one of the more curious and determined ones – some transform into something else."

"Transform into something like what?"

"Something like . . . *you,*" Linnea said with a shrug, then paused a moment and she and Milo both watched Axel intently.

Eventually Axel spoke. "So . . . suppose that in some bizarro universe this could ever be true – why is it important? Why did it come up now?"

"Because," Linnea continued, again taking hold of his thin, sickly arm. "The weaker your body becomes, the more your soul is able to shine through, whatever its source. By becoming less, you become more, if that makes sense." She paused again. "Have you ever watched anyone die?"

"No. People in my life die very unexpectedly and never *ever* where I can watch them actually do it."

"They radiate with inner light. A glow that shines bright as the sun. You can see it if you really look."

Axel wondered if he was glowing. A quick glance at his reflection in the window confirmed that he was rotting rather than radiating.

"You are, in essence, less and less physically Axel Hooley the sicker you become, and your spirit begins to emerge and become more and more. *That* is who you truly are. 'Axel Hooley' is just a shell you're walking around in this time around."

Little did Linnea know what a tenuous grip he had on being Axel Hooley in the first place. Still, he didn't find her outlined concept particularly reassuring. "What do you mean, 'this time around?'"

"Well," she said, glancing at Milo, without judgment, but with an apparent plea for support. "Depending on how many times you've lived before, of course."

Milo perked up and leaned in as if they were about to share secrets. "How many past lives has he had?"

"How many have you had, Milo?" Axel bellowed, wishing he had a means to escape this ridiculousness.

"Milo's had 17 or 18," Linnea said, matter-of-factly. "Depending on whether or not we count the newborn with the distended bowels, drowned by the midwife during the Franco-Prussian war. I suspect Milo didn't even bother to show up for that one."

"Linnea's had 34 past lives. She's ancient," Milo added smugly, as if the whole thing were a preposterous game that he couldn't stop himself from playing.

Axel, too, thought the idea was ridiculous, but he was having trouble resisting the pull of Linnea's alluring vortex. "Okay . . . so how many past lives have I had?"

Linnea looked as if she might scold Milo at any moment, but instead she sighed and shook her hands out. "Do you mind if I assess your energy?"

Axel didn't know what that might entail, so he just shrugged apprehensively.

"I'm very gentle."

"You're a whack-job," he muttered.

"Just be still a moment." Linnea held her palms toward him like they were Geiger counters trying to unearth buried treasure on the beach. She made a couple of grabbing motions in the air, then threw away whatever she snagged. Axel didn't feel anything. Linnea relaxed and looked Axel in the eye. "Four, I think. Almost certainly. Four." She nodded, as if to cement the definitiveness of the answer.

"I think four sounds like kind of a lot."

"Believe me, it isn't. You're practically a fetus compared with the rest of us. And yours are *all human,* which is highly unusual. Fascinating, really. When you're healthy, I'll bet you're really starting to get the hang of things, aren't you? You're lucky – a bewildered young soul can easily become a criminal or end up institutionalized or something."

"Give me time," Axel cautioned. "I'm not finished yet."

They sat quietly for a few minutes. Axel watched them nibble their crispy tofu and Thai garden rolls before he broke the silence. "How can you be so damn sure any of this is true?"

Linnea looked sad, and for the slightest moment appeared to be hundreds of years old. "I can tell by looking at you, Axel. Your dear little body is practically uninhabitable right now. Isn't it?"

They all knew she was right, but that didn't prove anything as far as Axel was concerned. "Can't this wait? Just a little while?

You know – until I get better?" Axel wanted to wait until he was sturdy enough to explain in articulate terms why they were both vicious nut-bags for dragging him out for this ridiculousness. He wasn't certain of Linnea's intent, but even if it were possible that she could be right, the idea of opening a door with so much potential for chaos and psychic disaster was overwhelming.

"What if you don't get better?" Milo said, slapping the theoretical cards that Linnea had so carefully laid out on the table. "What if, as ludicrous as it sounds, Linnea is right? If you don't make it, Axel, don't you at least want to know? I think knowing is always better."

"But you don't even believe it," Axel pointed out.

"Let's just say I'm a curious skeptic."

"Fuck you, Milo. I'm not a lab rat," Axel said, then corrected himself. "I'm not *your* lab rat, anyway." He was ready to bolt, but he didn't have the oomph to accomplish it quickly enough to have the desired effect. Linnea seemed to recognize this, so she nodded serenely and handed him her card.

Axel took the card. "I'm sorry, but I don't think I'm up for this nonsense. It won't help anything. I'm having enough trouble as it is."

"Of course you are." Linnea shook her head as if he were a lost child with little hope of finding his way back to civilization. "If you decide you need me, you'll call."

Axel shambled toward the exit, wanting nothing more than to get the hell out of there, but he heard Linnea call him, so he turned. *"What?!"* he demanded. "What, now?!"

"Nobody said anything," Milo responded, looking startled.

Linnea shed her jacket and rolled up the sleeve of her blouse far enough to reveal a half-sleeve of gorgeous tattoos winding their way up her arm. She clarified the move for Milo's benefit. "Axel was wondering if I had any tattoos. I have these vines. My 'bicep foliage.'"

"You have one more," Axel said. Or maybe he just thought he said it.

Linnea blushed and nodded. "Yes, but I'm having that one removed, you intrusive scamp."

Milo couldn't have looked more befuddled. "Who said anything about tattoos?"

Axel just nodded slowly and turned to go. He and Linnea understood each other, no matter who it is she might turn out to be. No matter who it is they might *both* turn out to be.

Right now he was all wrapped up in his efforts to remain Axel Hooley, at least for a little while longer. He just couldn't scare up the enthusiasm to be a mythical woodland creature, too.

# Chapter 18

## The Forest for the Trees

Axel dozed in Maude's car on the way back to Silverlake, waking whenever he felt her cool hand on his brow. He opened his eyes a couple of times to find Maude's beautiful, thick, ebony hand holding onto his slender, translucent arm. He smiled drowsily, and felt that perhaps she was trying to force some of her strength of spirit into him.

When they got back to Dale's, she limped up to the house to see who was available to help Axel make the trip. Maude still walked with a cane, resulting from her car accident; and just getting up the steps was all she could manage on her own. After a few minutes, Rhymey hustled down from the house, opened the car door, scooped Axel into his arms, and bounded back up the stairs two at a time.

Axel sat in the living room under a quilt and listened to Maude, Rhymey, and Zoë chatter away over a bottle of wine. Maude was well versed in religion, art, culture, and world politics, but if she wasn't lecturing, she tended to spend her efforts serenely learning about others rather than displaying her own broad range of scholarship. She talked with Rhymey about his Amish childhood in Pennsylvania, and they laughed at his stories of the challenging, yet theoretically uncomplicated lives he and Axel had left so very far behind.

"I could have told you all about the Amish if you wanted to know, Maudie," Axel offered. "I just can't imagine why you give a shit."

"Maybe I want the culture without the venom, Mister G-String." Maude retorted, to the delight of both Zoë and Rhymey. Axel suddenly felt a little sad at the idea that the innocuous depravity of his stripper days were over, which was so ridiculous that he figured the chemo was probably fucking with his brain again.

Zoë walked him into the den to help him get ready for bed. He desperately wanted to take a couple of OxyContin to knock himself out, but was afraid that if he did, the approaching fevers might not wake him up in time to get to the hospital if that turned out to be what he needed.

Zoë offered to sleep within earshot in the living room, but Axel insisted that wasn't necessary and she should return to the comfort and luxury of Dale's upstairs bed. Rhymey could sleep in the living room if he wanted to, as he seemed to be spending most of his time at Dale's anyway. Besides, Axel was perfectly capable of calling for assistance if he needed it, at least for now.

Axel closed his eyes, not really anticipating sleep, but hoping that he might zone out enough to get a little rest. He figured he had been laying there for several hours by the time all hell broke loose.

$\emptyset$  $\emptyset$  $\emptyset$

The explosion was more violent than a ruptured gas line, even a large one, might have detonated. If the hillside on which Dale's house perched had consisted of gunpowder, ignited by a cigarette from some careless smoker, it would only have resulted in a small fraction of the violence Axel experienced as he shot up into the air. The only rational explanation for such force likely involved the complete and utter spontaneous combustion of the entire planet.

Axel blasted upward from the volcanic, primordial charge which must certainly have originated deep within the Earth beneath his warm sofa bed in Dale's comfy den. The searing pain was palpable, yet impossible to isolate. It was highly unlikely that the shards of his shattered body had been able to accompany his consciousness at such velocity. The scattered leftovers of Axel Hooley thus accelerated upward through the starry landscape and into the unknown.

Any sense of time that had ever once existed had blown to smithereens, along with all the people and energy bars and dogs and imported Spanish tile and strip malls. Axel fought to remain conscious for as long as he could, but quickly lost track of how much time had elapsed. Seconds and centuries seemed strangely like the exact same thing. His very being was burning the last of itself, scorching away as he accelerated.

There was no sense in fighting it, and besides, he had no strength left with which to do so. So Axel pleaded with the Universe to continue on without him and let him go. He hoped that whatever currents existed, wherever he was, would have the cosmic decency to finish him off quickly and without further pain.

As Axel heaved his last surrender, he felt a gentle grip enfold him with its tranquil, even embrace. He was reminded of the compression garments that he'd seen patients wear back at Cedars-Sinai all those thousands of years ago – the ones that held everything securely in place. The pain subsided, but then he couldn't recall exactly how or when it had taken its leave. The force surrounding him kept him safe, and he understood that it would stay with him during his journey. Journey? How did he know he was on a journey? Or even that there was a destination, necessarily?

Tommy! It was Tommy surrounding him, he suddenly realized. Tommy, beside him and around him and within him and they were soaring as one, unimpeded through the purple and blue sky. *This* is what Axel had been trying to reproduce, in his clumsy way, with the primitive hang gliders back in Zion. The sensation was so complete, familiar, and totally inborn that his mortal form must have gone mad trying to rediscover it with a cumbersome, man-made, unwieldy aluminum and nylon hang glider. No wonder they had failed so miserably! This, in fact, was exactly how and what it was *supposed* to be. The relief at realizing that his folly hadn't been the solitary cause of Tommy's death was overwhelming for a moment, and then immediately seemed so far away that feeling at all concerned about it was ridiculous.

Axel felt Rachel and Tad McKenna merge with and then surround him. There were others, too, but his overstimulated mind couldn't clearly distinguish identities. He was encapsulated by love and radiance and complete acceptance and fulfillment. Nothing he had ever known or felt or imagined or dreamt could compare. It seemed impossible that such divine perfection could exist.

He abruptly burst upward, propelled forth by the strength of his fellow voyagers, and floated free and independent, gently suspended in time and space. He felt wonderfully at peace. He must be dead – it was the only explanation. He tried to remember if he was supposed to go *into* the light or go *away from* the light, but no light had yet presented itself or demanded that he make a choice, so he just enjoyed the sensation and didn't worry about it.

For whatever reason, he couldn't seem to accomplish any sort of physical inventory. He thought for a moment that he had somehow plugged back into the strong and agile body of his former, pre-cancer self, and then immediately rejected the idea. Whatever he'd morphed into, it was far better than anything he had ever been. He was powerful – Beautiful beyond imagination – Magnificent – Majestic – God-like. He was everyone and everything and every dream, thought, or idea. He was connected. And what's more, this wasn't his first time at the party.

Suddenly, a presence washed over him like a tidal wave, which felt amazing as he united with it. It was so warm and understanding and loving. He was clearly a part of it and they were part of everything else – together, yet somehow his individuality held strong. Axel suddenly understood – a bazillion synapses fired simultaneously – he understood – *Everything.* This was not a question and answer forum. There was just knowing and understanding. There would never be sufficient words in any language or any image known to man to ever explain this, so Axel tried very hard to will himself to remember the feeling, as impossible as that might be.

He understood that the experiences he was ultimately supposed to have would indeed be had, yet even with this feeling of predestination, he didn't feel robbed of his individuality or his ability to make choices. There was an inherent rightness to everything – A rightness to his very existence, though moment by moment he may not appear to be who he wanted, intended, or expected himself to be in the smaller, human sense.

He held it, sparking and glorious and beautiful – the answers to the why and how of everything he'd ever failed to understand. It was amazing – like a glowing, beautiful crystal that extended outward forever. He understood the complex, intertwined relationships of everyone he'd surrounded himself with. How they fit together so beautifully and impacted each other, exerting influences for their mutual good, even if a momentary intent was less than noble. The apparent randomness wasn't without a far-reaching design, spanning eons as individual threads intertwined and wove a tapestry of which he was most certainly a part. Axel recognized his own thread and how it fit into the weave – it was a relatively new addition to the motif, but no less important, and it extended onward farther than he could comprehend – and the way it wound around the others was so artful and stunning that he was overwhelmed with emotion contemplating the staggering immensity of it all.

Then suddenly everything shattered. The brilliant, sparkling, delicate crystallized answers to the riddle of life and the universe shattered to pieces. He had the sensation of scrambling, grasping for something, anything – a shard he could take with him. Something important to have. Something he could know. *Something.*

Just then, his being lost contact with all sense of buoyancy and hope. He had no choice but to accept the inevitable, so he rolled and power dived, leaden, and overwhelmed by a sense of dread. His head spun and the familiar pain and nausea settled back into his being. He had no doubt – he was going back to the ruined shell of the second Axel Hooley that was dying slowly by degree in a tiny room in Dale Oakley's warm, tastefully decorated home on the hill. Back to the pain and despair and anger and the inconsolable loneliness. Back to his fake, but familiar identity and his messy, awful, decimated life.

At some point, it occurred to him that he ought to make an effort to locate his physical body. He was confident that they would come across each other eventually, but he preferred they hook up at Dale's place rather than a tree in Beverly Hills or somewhere even less desirable. Obviously, some kind of homing signal was coming from somewhere, so he tried to concentrate as he plummeted in order to detect where it was coming from.

He recognized that this was the part he had never really gotten the hang of.

# Chapter 19

## A Tree Grows in Silverlake

Zoë kept her hand on Rhymey's back so that she could feel his rhythms as he slept and attempt to synch her breath with his, albeit unsuccessfully. Aside from the obvious motive, they hadn't tiptoed upstairs together for any particular reason besides the notion that secrecy made their whole assignation feel more clandestine and exciting. It's not as if their sleeping together mattered to Axel, at least not beyond the merciless ribbing he would give them whenever he found out about it. Tonight's tryst wasn't planned, by any stretch of the imagination, and Zoë couldn't further imagine it would be ongoing, at least not for very long. Still, it was nice, and felt absolutely essential just a few hours ago. Besides, Rhymey was a real *guy*, lumbering and robust and very unlike the legal and finance geeks she usually ran across then ended up avoiding for weeks or months at a time until they finally took the hint and stopped calling.

*Team Axel* had been confronted with a sense of their own mortality, whether they liked it or not, and had collectively begun living in and for the moment. By morning, Zoë would blame the whole escapade on those damn brownies. Rhymey always avoided all manner of drugs and alcohol, as did Zoë, generally, if you didn't count the occasional glass of wine, or two, or three.

And it wasn't as if the odd tasting baked goods Cheryl regularly delivered weren't awfully suspicious to begin with, or that Zoë had been so naïve as to believe they hadn't been enhanced. But Zoë found sleeping in a strange bed to be awkward, dealing with Axel was stressful, and the randomness of cancer was fraying her nerves; so the goddamned brownies, cupcakes, and pharmaceutical-quality hash just threw a cozy blanket of calm over everything.

Rhymey was backwards in all the ways Axel had overcome because of the advantages of education, but he didn't have Axel's angst or baggage either, and that was certainly worth something. Both country boys approached the world in a generally open, somewhat naïve way that Zoë both envied and ridiculed, but Rhymey had yet to repel her in any of the grinding and crazy Axel-esque ways. Unlike Axel, who always managed to seem lost in the wilderness, Rhymey had long ago figured out the world and carved himself a unique and comfortable place in it.

She wondered briefly if Rhymey was a heavy sleeper. The manlier men often were, or so she believed, not having taken as much of a survey as she would have liked. Zoë continued to stare at the ceiling, concerned that perhaps Rhymey was still Amish enough to believe they were engaged or about to jump the broom or some such nonsense as a result of their woozy, passionate rampage. As was the case with most men, she had no idea what was going through his mind, so she beat each and every possibility to death in hers. Although Zoë may or may not be an actual tigress in the bedroom, she'd certainly put her sexual prowess up against your garden-variety Amish girl any day of the week, assuming of course that's what Rhymey was accustomed to, which may not actually be the case, come to think of it. At least that certainly wasn't the case since his arrival in Los Angeles, though she wasn't certain exactly how long ago that might have been. Rehashing it all was pointless anyway – they were all just doing the best they could to alleviate their tensions to whatever degree possible. Either that, or this really was something true and important and good that would eventually blow up in her face over what would most likely amount to nothing more than simple, petty trivialities. None of this was an issue just now, however, because the skylight above the bed had abruptly shattered.

Zoë screamed and flung herself protectively over Rhymey as a howling animal crashed into the bedroom from above. She immediately questioned her own protective impulse – it's not as if her lithe frame provided any sort of effective defense against a rabid bobcat or coyote, or even that she should necessarily feel responsible for shielding Rhymey. Whatever the creature was, it was terrified and in pain, and completely unlike any beast she'd ever heard. She hoped it would run off as quickly as it appeared, assuming that the addled thing hadn't mistaken them for easy prey. The position of Dale's house, nestled into the hill, was perfect for any adventurous animal driven down the mountain in search of leftovers, water, or small house pets to feed on.

The second howl confirmed her worst fears – whatever it was had fled downstairs in search of something it would certainly find – a defenseless meal that couldn't put up a fight.

Zoë leapt out of bed dragging Rhymey behind her. "*Axel!*" Just screaming his name, followed by an expletive spoke volumes, or at least it should have. Rhymey plunked off onto the floor where he rolled over and resumed his peaceful snooze, so she kicked her way out of the duvet cover and bedskirt, all the while cursing Dale and his elaborate gay bedding.

She crashed out onto the upstairs landing, stubbed her toe hard, and tumbled down the stairs swearing and extending whatever limbs she could in order to break her fall. She hoped nothing was broken besides the toe, which was definitely a lost cause, but she didn't have time to stop to check.

She limped through the living room and skidded into Axel's den on an area rug. The room was wrecked – furniture in disarray and violent scribbling all over the walls – disjointed, incoherent confusion that didn't make any sort of immediate sense. Unable to grasp the specifics because her eye was immediately drawn to a trail of blood leading down the hall, Zoë caught her balance and sped onward, praying she wasn't too late.

When she rounded the corner into the bathroom, Zoë couldn't believe what she saw – a tree thrust up from beneath the bathroom floor and was growing, powering upward at an alarming rate, right before her eyes, branches and tendrils spiraling up and up through the . . . that certainly didn't make any sense – there was open sky where the ceiling, and then presumably the upstairs, should have been. A thousand lights danced and flickered in its branches, whizzing around as if compelled by conscious inspiration. It occurred to Zoë that she had stumbled into some ancient place and then, also, that she was wearing the only outfit God gave her. Odd as it was, there felt a kind of appropriateness to it. The setting was so primal and elemental, she guessed this is how Eve must have felt, marveling at creation, or Alice, tumbling down the rabbit hole.

The rapidly spreading branches abruptly burst into bloom as if on command, and the tiny orbs of light intensified and danced in response, as if in celebration of her arrival. The tree then twisted its gnarled trunk and, as she had to remind herself later, seemed to actually peer directly at her. Awestruck, Zoë reached her hand up toward the boughs, unsure why, exactly, she was being so bold. A single branch responded in kind, extending a flowering vine which wrapped itself around her arm and then her torso in a tender embrace.

Zoë's head swam. In her last moment of cognizance before she swooned to the natural stone floor of Dale's guest bathroom, Zoë vowed that she wouldn't allow her mind to transform this phenomenon into a dream. This was, in every way, the most real thing she'd ever experienced, and she'd be damned if she'd allow it to be compromised.

# Chapter 20

## Consequential Dormancy

The front door was standing wide open as Dale dragged his luggage up onto the porch. He wasn't worried, particularly – an intruder would have to be exceptionally committed to breach his threshold and risk confronting Axel's legion of squatters. The alarm hadn't been activated either, which was also no surprise or cause for concern, necessarily. A house with so many bohemian inhabitants wasn't much in need of electronic warning.

The kitchen and the living room were in reasonable order, probably thanks to the efforts of Esperanza or Rhymey, or both. The den was another story altogether, however – Axel's nameless art deco greyhound had been pulverized, with splinters and sawdust strewn about the room. The walls were graffiti-covered with scrawled, nonsensical writing everywhere – *This is real! Real! Real! Real! It happened! We are part of everything! There are answers! Together we exist!*

The copious exclamation points somehow made the scene feel even more surreal and unsettling, like a museum installation by an angry, terrified artist without a firm grasp on reality, or any awareness of the liberating alternatives afforded by a broader color palette or modicum of punctuation restraint.

Dale failed to conjure up any sort of plausible scenario to explain the state of the den and couldn't begin to intuit what may have transpired. The evidence of something catastrophic and perhaps even whimsical was undeniable, but without any useful specifics to go on, he was clueless. He briefly considered getting angry, but didn't bother to expend the effort.

Axel didn't answer his phone, and neither did Zoë, so Dale tried Partho, also without any luck. His call to Rhymey went to the voicemail of a woman named Irisa, who sounded Slavic. He went to the kitchen where the Death Watch List was tacked up and proceeded to dial randomly through the remaining list.

Tyrell answered on the second ring, which made Dale suspect that he was still dealing drugs rather than responding quickly out of concern for Axel or the wayward youth to whom he alleged to minister. Tyrell hadn't heard from Axel, but provided Rhymey's correct cell phone number, which Axel had apparently mistyped.

Dale had only met two people who had ever been Amish, and they both owned mobile phones – probably a sign he should start preparing for the apocalypse.

Rhymey's grumbled hello sounded sluggish and tired, but that could be misleading. Dale had always found Rhymey to be plodding and methodical, which obliged him to question whether he himself was becoming too much of an impatient American, heaven forbid.

"Rhymey? This is Dale."

"Well, hullo there, Dale!" Rhymey sounded pleased and oddly surprised. "How are things up there in Winnipeg?"

"Fine, I suppose, though I was only there one time when I was eight. I just got back from Vancouver. Listen, do you know where Axel is? Or Zo? I think something may have happened—"

"Ayuh. I'm here with our Zoë in her hospital room right now."

"*Zoë's* in the hospital?"

"That she is, Dale. She found Axel after he passed over."

"Passed over?" Dale wheezed, as if he'd been punched in the gut. *"Axel's dead?"*

"No, no, no! So sorry, Dale, I misspoke. He passed *out*. I'm mixing my 'keeling *over*' with my 'passing *out*.' So much is going on right now. We're all very tired."

Rhymey was generally charming in an oafish sort of way, but he was leaning fiercely on Dale's last nerve. "So Axel's alright then, eh?"

"He's in intensive care. Things don't look very good for our Axel right now, my friend."

Dale rubbed the bridge of his nose. There had always been room for everyone in Axel's world, which was admirable on the one hand, and utterly maddening on the other. In a land so haphazardly inclusive, nobody but Axel himself could truly feel comfortable.

"So, what happened to Zoë?"

"Zoë had herself a spell and broke her toe."

"A *spell?* What kind of spell?"

"Our poor Zoë fell to the vapors."

Dale figured nobody had actually suffered from the vapors since the late nineteenth century, and even then only in Southern Gothic literature. He counted to 10 as he waited patiently for Rhymey to elaborate.

"When your skylight crashed in, Zoë hurried downstairs to be with Axel. By the time I got down there, they were both lying on the bathroom floor naked."

"The skylight?" Dale took the stairs two at a time, astounded by the amount of damage his tidy household could sustain during the few days he'd been absent. He hurried into the room and looked up at the skylight which, to his great relief, was intact and completely undamaged. The bedding was in disarray and some clothing was strewn about; otherwise, there was no evidence of destruction.

"The skylight looks alright, Rhymey," Dale said. "Every-thing's fine."

"Oh?" Rhymey said, sounding genuinely surprised. "I reckon I didn't look at it myself. Zoë told the ambulance doctor that a wild animal came through it." Rhymey paused again. "The ambulance people would like you to install an escalator for the hill, by the way."

"Alright," Dale agreed, distractedly. "Wait a minute – did you say they were *naked?*"

"Ayah. That they were. I averted my eyes as best I could."

"Why would Axel take his clothes off?"

"I'm sure I wouldn't know, Dale," Rhymey insisted, with a twinge of defensiveness. "Why does Axel do *anything?*"

"That's fair," Dale acknowledged. "Zoë was naked, too?"

Rhymey was silent for so long that Dale thought perhaps they had lost their connection. Finally, he spoke. "I believe our Zoë may have started her day that way."

"Have the doctors told you anything?" Dale still wasn't certain to what degree illness and injury had taken their toll, so he gathered his things together to head out the door as he spoke.

"They only have authority to speak with you or Zoë, and the vapors seem to have driven Zoë and her senses toward two different picnic tables."

"Look, I'm on my way. Are you alright? Is there anything you need, Rhymey?"

"Just speaking with somebody pleasant who has their wits about them has been a real treat, Dale. I will look forward to seeing you."

"Thanks, Rhymey," Dale hung up. Axel's doctors were all on speed dial, so he phoned on the way back to his car.

Axel's Oncologist, Dr. Kenn, confirmed that Axel was comatose resulting from his body's violent reaction to the chemo and his high fever. Beyond the bloodcurdling sound of the word *comatose*, the ongoing state of unconsciousness wasn't considered dire all by itself, however. At least not yet. They were keeping Axel packed in ice to push his fever down and had disconnected his chemotherapy infusion unit. They suspected that his PICC line was infected too, so he was receiving antibiotics.

Better that Axel was unaware of all this activity – being cheated out of the full dose of chemotherapy would have infuriated him. He was doing all his homework, after all, yet failing his exams anyway. Axel could heal a day or two free from pain and discomfort, and that was certainly for the best.

Lying quiet and dormant isn't such a bad thing, Dale told himself. It's what even the heartiest plants do in winter, and they eventually manage to spring back to life. Axel would, too. Maybe.

The drive from Silverlake to Cedars-Sinai was uneventful and without much traffic, which gave Dale the opportunity to do the heavy thinking he'd long been avoiding. Worst-case scenarios haunted every mile of the brief trip. His hands hadn't trembled this badly since the drive to Utah to claim Tommy's beautiful but broken body.

There were those who had expected Dale to despise Axel, and were unquestionably disappointed when he didn't, not the least of whom was Axel himself. Dale couldn't bring himself to do so of course, and even if he'd wanted to, he wasn't capable of hating Axel more than Axel hated himself. And anyway, such efforts would have ultimately cheated them both out of the friendship they needed in order to bear such a loss. It occurred to Dale that maybe the cancer was meant to fulfill some subconscious need Axel had to punish himself and atone for Tommy's death? He didn't believe in that sort of thing, really, but the timing of events could certainly be interpreted to support such a conclusion.

With Tommy gone, Dale was closer to Axel than any remaining soul on Earth, which he found to be an astonishing flash of insight. Axel wasn't his link to Tommy – he never truly had been. Dale couldn't go on pretending that's all he was. Using Axel as a memorial bridge to Tommy was a sedative of his own invention – a self-defense mechanism designed to keep him from cracking up if Axel didn't make it. The elastic bond between Axel and Dale existed entirely on its own and always had – it stretched beyond all reasonable limits when Tommy died, and if it didn't break then, it just wasn't ever going to.

Dale was perfectly capable of losing something as trifling as a link to somebody he'd loved and forever lost, if it came to that. What he unequivocally could not do right now was lose somebody important. Certainly not Axel. And most definitely not today.

# Chapter 21

## A Vigil at Cedars

When Zoë came out from under sedation, she argued with Rhymey, insulted a nurse, and checked herself out of the hospital, insisting that she was perhaps the only truly sane person who had ever lived. Hospital regulations strictly required patients being released to be pushed out to the curb in a wheelchair by an orderly, whether they liked it or not.

Once outside, Zoë stood up from her wheelchair, turned on her heels, walked back into the hospital, and took the elevator up to the Intensive Care Unit where Axel's entourage had already begun to converge in the lounge.

Claude and Cheryl were making a fuss over how grown-up Partho looked, though they'd only known the boy a couple of months. "Probably all the responsibility he's taken on, looking after Axel and all," Cheryl assured the assembled Death Watchers, even as she turned her attention back to Partho.

"Yes, Axel would be lost without you," Sylvia chimed in. "Your people have always been so gentle and caring."

"My *people?*" Partho asked, trying to decide if it was time to be offended.

"Of course, dear. Your 'people.' Your 'tribe.'"

"I'm *East* Indian," Partho sputtered. "Not *Woo-Woo* Indian."

Sylvia chuckled, having apparently achieved the reaction she was after. "We're all from a tribe, dear. Some tribes are just more lost than others. Even Axel hails from a tribe, though as far as anybody knows, he may have hatched from an Easter egg." Sylvia patted Partho's leg affectionately and smiled. "It must be fun for you boys to drive around in your little Posh Boxers."

*"Porsche Boxster!"* Partho corrected, coming to terms with the fact that battles with Sylvia were generally unwinnable.

Zoë determined that if she eavesdropped much longer, she'd start smashing skulls together, so she leaned on the sofa and whispered to Dale. "Have you seen him?"

"Not yet. You have to be next of kin to visit someone in a coma."

"We pay his bills – we're next of kin." Zoë made her way down the ICU hall with Dale hurrying after her.

Axel was hooked up to several intravenous drip bags with plastic tubing running in and out of his PICC line, a vein in his hand and most every available orifice. Zoë winced at the sight of his skin, which varied from alabaster white to a bruised and sickly yellowish beige. Neither of them said anything for a long time, though Dale did put his arm around her once she began to cry.

Between quiet sobs, Zoë managed to squeak a few words into Dale's shoulder "I need to tell you something."

"Okay" Dale nodded, though he didn't sound as if he really wanted to hear it. "Whenever you're ready."

"It's crazy. Really and truly crazy."

"I'm good with crazy. Better lately, in fact."

Zoë looked up at him pleadingly, with her wet, blue eyes. "Yes, but this is Axel-Hooley-to-the-ninth-power-bugass-batshit-crazy. Crazy from Axel and crazy from me are two vastly different things."

"Oh?"

"If Axel tells you something bugass-batshit-crazy, it's because Axel *is* bugass-batshit-crazy." Zoë broke into another sob. "But if I tell you something's bugass-batshit-crazy, you'd damn well better believe that things truly *are* bugass-batshit-crazy!"

"Go ahead and tell me," Dale said gently, preparing himself for Zoë's bugass-batshit-craziest.

So Zoë told Dale everything – the howling, wounded animal crashing through the skylight, breaking her toe on the landing, the trail of blood in the downstairs den, the tree in the bathroom that seemed to look at her, and how it burst into bloom with the dancing lights in its branches – everything. She was grateful to repeat it all aloud because the experience already felt like it was slipping away at 100 miles an hour. The only tangible proof she could produce was her broken toe in the soft-boot cast. When she finished, she took a deep breath. "And it was all real. Absolutely real. Everything."

"Gee," Dale said, failing in his effort not to sound skeptical. "Everything?"

"Before I lost consciousness, the tree . . . spoke."

Dale nodded and cupped his hand over his mouth in what he hoped looked like an expression of awe rather than the stifling of anything inappropriate.

"It said something I didn't understand. Two words, or a two-part phrase. I think it was some kind of ancient language."

"It's too bad you don't speak *magic tree*," Dale said, then coughed to conceal his bemusement.

"Yes," Zoë nodded, daring him to refute her tale, though her eyes conceded how that might be difficult. "So you see, the whole thing really *is* bugass-batshit-crazy."

Axel's right eye unexpectedly pried itself open and focused on Zoë with apparent effort. He tugged his oxygen line from his face and held her gaze. Finally, he spoke in a wheezing, exhausted tone. "That was no animal – it was *me* . . . Dipshit."

"Shhhh. You need to rest," Zoë whispered in her best soothing manner. "And don't bite the hand that may eventually be forced to unplug your sorry ass."

Axel dropped his head back and it lolled to the side, drowsily. "You and Rhymey in bed . . . utter chaos . . . dogs and cats, Amish and Agnostics, inappropriate copulating as far as the eye can see." Axel's eye briefly twinkled and then closed. Then he began to drool. Zoë gently maneuvered his oxygen back into place.

"Oh?" Dale's eyebrows snapped skyward. "You and Rhymey? For real?" Dale asked, although the facts were verified by Zoë's reaction. "So . . . is Rhymey cut or uncut?"

"I'm about ready to smack you."

"Oh, so *now* you're a prude?" Zoë threw Dale a scowl, so he just shrugged and continued. "Anyway, the skylight wasn't broken. The only thing that's going to require any attention are the Percales, the design of which has been discontinued, by the way, but I think a little all-fabric bleach will take care of that."

"Rhymey and I were just—"

"Violating the sanctity of my bed?" Dale interrupted, not that he cared. His bed hadn't had its sanctity violated in a good long while. He was just grateful that somebody had gone ahead and done it.

Zoë sighed and settled back in her chair, keeping her eyes on Axel in case he showed further signs of life. "So maybe it was Axel instead of a wild animal and maybe the skylight was open or something. I may be a bit foggy with the details, but I can't imagine how he got up on your roof in the first place, or why. The more I think about it, the more I'm convinced it was a dream and not a real experience at all. Maybe I dreamed up Rhymey, too?" Zoë paused, as if wrestling with her own psyche. "No – this is just something my brain is doing to save me from years of therapy. It was all definitely real, no matter what I say next." Zoë sniffed back a tear and rested her head on Dale's shoulder. "And I'm going to have to say it was a dream because I just can't manage to hold onto it any other way. I'll go crazy if I have to try and keep this real."

"It sounds like the same dream Tommy had," Dale offered, but quickly regretted.

"Sleeping Beauty seems to have given up the ghost," Zoë nodded once to indicate that he should proceed. "I've got nothing but time, so don't hold anything back."

Dale sighed, understanding that resistance wouldn't be worth the trouble. "It was the night before Tommy and Axel left Vegas.

Tommy was completely drunk and a couple of guys were beating him up in an alley, so I don't think Tommy's version of events can be considered particularly reliable."

Zoë opened her arms to indicate that she was still all ears, so Dale dug in and tried to remember the tale as best he could, though he worried that divulging Tommy's harrowing saga was a violation of some kind of trust. "Tommy said that one of the guys bashing him had raised a hunting knife ready to drive it into his throat. He could see Axel running down the alley toward him, but he was afraid he wouldn't get there in time . . ."

"Oh my God," Zoë gasped as if the danger were immediate and Tommy hadn't died of equally violent and completely unrelated causes many months ago. "What happened?"

"This is Tommy's bugass-batshit-crazy part . . ." Dale looked as if he wanted to forget the whole thing, but he knew he was already in too deep.

"Go on," Zoë insisted.

Dale fixed his eyes on Axel and continued the bizarre odyssey. "He said that Axel flew. He lifted up off his feet – actually *flew* – his body focused and transformed . . ."

"*Transformed?*"

"Yes – Tommy described him as a *supernova firefly.*" Dale nearly choked on the absurdity of his words. "He shot forward and melted the hunting knife right there in the guy's hand."

Zoë tried to picture Axel as a heroic spotlight swooping in to save the day, but the only image she could bring into focus was a vaguely masculine Tinker Bell. "Wow," Zoë mumbled, though Dale couldn't tell whether she sounded skeptical or not.

"Then the light shot up into the air and came down hard, driving deep into the earth right there in the middle of the alley."

Zoë nodded, obviously still intrigued. "And?"

"And . . ." Dale continued, with a defeated groan. Zoë was going to dog him until he finished, so he might as well get it over with. "According to Tommy, a lightning storm blew in – and remember this was Nevada where I don't think they even *have* lightning storms – and a giant oak tree shot up out of the ground, hurling the men around in its branches, both screaming like the devil." Dale flushed bright red and shook his head. "Have I mentioned how completely hammered Tommy was that night?"

Zoë shrugged, defiantly. "So? I was knocked on my ass by hash brownies. That doesn't mean *my* experience wasn't real."

"Tommy believed that the tree in his dream . . . because, you understand, he was drunk and terrified and hurt, so it obviously had to be a dream – Tommy said that the tree and the supernova firefly and maybe even the lightning storm were all manifestations of Axel." Dale sat back and relaxed into his chair, feeling somewhat relieved. "Tommy also reiterated that it was, without a doubt, a dream."

"So what happened to the two guys?"

"Right," Dale nodded, as he was inevitably sucked back in. "The men were unconscious, and when Axel returned to normal, he didn't remember any of it. He took the attacker with the melted hand to the emergency room, or that's what he said he did, anyway. He wasn't gone very long, according to Tommy, so maybe he just tossed the body in a dumpster or something?"

"How can you be sure it was a dream? How could Tommy know for sure?"

"What else could it be? It's the only explanation."

"Look, Axel has his shortcomings – *plenty* of shortcomings. But we both know he's incapable of causing any real harm – the absolute worst he can manage is temporary chaos on a minor, interpersonal level." Zoë paused. "And he doesn't exactly have the wherewithal to go around disposing of bodies, either." After further reflection, Zoë finished with an undeniable conclusion. "*I* could hide a body. If push came to shove, I think even *you* could hide a body. But not Axel – he isn't that vicious, clever or capable."

"Probably not," Dale agreed. "Maybe that's why God keeps turning him into an enchanted tree?"

✆ ✆ ✆

Dr. Kenn briefed Zoë and Dale and the rest of the assembled Death Watchers on Axel's condition just after lunch. His appraisal was solemn, and a number of grim possibilities were presented, discussed, then awkwardly dismissed. Only Sylvia, the grande dame of the group, remained resolute. "We appreciate your assessment, doctor, but that boy is going to make it if I have to rip the heart out of my chest and pump his goddamn blood all by myself."

Dale began organizing a chart in order for the Death Watchers to alternate shifts at Axel's bedside. Zoë and a few others felt this was excessive, but nobody complained because putting things in order was Dale's way of coping. Partho talked his way into the ICU by convincing one of the Intensive Care nurses that he was Axel's son, flown in from Calcutta years ago for a trendy Hollywood adoption.

Linnea arrived at Cedars-Sinai midafternoon with Milo on her arm and an icepack on her head, having phoned the hospital based on significantly more than a hunch. Following a brief discussion with the nurse at the intake desk, she staggered over to Dale, who was demonstrating the apps on his mobile device for Zoë and Partho.

"You're with Axel Hooley? Sorry to interrupt. I'm Linnea."

"What?" Zoë said looking up, somewhat alarmed. "I mean, *who?*"

"Linnea," she repeated. "Linnea Fanshaw."

"Oh my God," Zoë said, looking as if she'd seen a ghost.

"Who?" Dale asked, rising to his feet in to either greet the woman or throw a protective barrier around Zoë, whichever was required.

Zoë stood and repeated the name, as if trying the words out. "Linnea Fanshaw? *Linnea Fanshaw!*" She turned to Dale excitedly. "That's what the tree said – 'Linnea Fanshaw!'"

"You talk to trees?" Milo inquired, as he slipped his arm casually around Linnea.

Linnea introduced Milo and explained that he was Axel's hypnotherapist, which was a surprise to everyone but Partho.

Then she introduced herself again, suggesting that she was a friend and that Axel had called for her.

"He's been in a coma all day," Zoë said, still wary of the two strangers. "Axel can't even call for a bedpan. He couldn't have called for you or anybody else."

Linnea shrugged and removed the icepack from her forehead, revealing one reddened eye that had nearly swollen shut. "Apparently he didn't have access to a land line."

"When I couldn't reach her, I drove over to her place," Milo interjected, with an irrelevant air of self-importance. "She was unconscious on her bathroom floor."

"Yes, I hear that's going around," Zoë added, without elaborating.

Linnea inserted herself on the sofa between Zoë and Dale, leaving Milo to scramble for a chair.

"Linnea's psychic," Milo said, though it was clear from Linnea's inelegant glance that she didn't appreciate his assistance. "Sometimes she connects with people," he offered, apologetically. "Right now, she's apparently tuned in to *Radio Axel.*"

It took Linnea roughly 20 minutes of hasty explanation to persuade the Death Watchers that she was for real, at least to some extent. Even after Linnea's detailed enlightenment and Zoë's troubling recognition of her name, they weren't nearly convinced of what she believed to be Axel's bona fide origins, or the concept that his dryad soul might be thrashing its way out of his ailing body and going out on excursions. Zoë worried that perhaps the tree had belched forth the name as some sort of macabre warning, and both she and Dale remained doubtful, though intrigued enough to share their two tall tales of two tall trees.

"This is ridiculous," Dale laughed nervously, once they reached an inevitable uncomfortable silence.

"I don't know, Dale," Zoë said, compelling herself to consider every nonsensical possibility. "We never did find out how he ended up in Beverly Hills that morning."

"Even if astral projection were possible, how could his physical body end up all the way across town?" Dale asked, his arms crossed defiantly.

Linnea just shook her head. "He isn't strong. Not physically, anyway – he's not grounded. If his body was somehow dragged off to intercept his soul, it speaks volumes with regard to Axel's spirit." A look of intense sorrow clouded Linnea's face as she continued. "I don't know what it says about the survival of his corporeal being, but my feeling is the situation is dire."

"This is ridiculous," Dale repeated, though mildly impressed with Linnea's use of vocabulary.

"Axel knows things!" Partho piped up, obviously captivated by all the new data. "He knows things he doesn't have any business knowing. He wasn't like that until he got sick."

"It's true," Milo nodded. "I can't vouch for what he was like before, but Axel intuits things. *Personal* things. I'm not certain that he's aware of how much he's pulling out of us, necessarily." Milo caught Partho's eye, and they turned their single-minded gaze toward Dale. "He just knows."

"These aren't likely conscious choices for Axel," Linnea surmised, hesitantly. "They only seem to happen when he's in distress – a great deal of distress."

Zoë and Dale briefly waited for further convincing, but Linnea was done rationalizing her presence. Zoë sighed. "Alright – If Axel turns into a wood nymph, why didn't I *see* a wood nymph? All I saw was a tree and some fireflies."

"You saw what you saw because you are able to comprehend trees and fireflies," Linnea said, not unkindly. "Don't take this the wrong way, but – I suspect that a wood nymph is slightly beyond your grasp. Humans see hamadryads as tiny orbs of light, if they can see them at all, which is unlikely."

"Like Tinker Bell," Zoë whispered quietly to herself.

"Or a supernova firefly," Dale added, with a touch of irony.

Linnea smiled and arched the brow over her good eye. "Something like that, yes."

"That makes some sense, at least," Dale said. "When Columbus first landed, the native Americans weren't able to see

140

his three ships – they just couldn't fathom something that big floating out on the ocean. Their minds couldn't comprehend tall ships, so they didn't see any."

"How is it you know more weird crap about American history than I do?" Zoë asked.

Dale shrugged. "I blame your inferior educational system."

Linnea and Milo accompanied Zoë and Partho to the hospital cafeteria while Dale went to assume his shift at Axel's bedside in order to give Tyrell and Esperanza a break.

∅ ∅ ∅

The Death Watchers came and went over the next two days. Some were a more constant presence than others, but everybody managed to make an appearance most every day. They proceeded with the bare bones of their daily lives, to whatever extent was minimally required. Milo and Linnea joined their numbers without fanfare, and collectively they began pushing each other's hot-buttons. As each hour passed without Axel awakening, they inevitably took turns standing strong, sniping at each other, breaking down, and ultimately providing comfort and assurance.

No one but Maude ever actually saw Partho cry, but late one night his red, puffy eyes exposed his lack of sufficient teenage machismo. His grief wasn't only for Axel, of course, but for the mother who he hardly knew and had never, until recently, given much thought.

"Baby, those tears have to come out," Maude assured him when the two were alone "May as well let 'em fly while Maudie's here with a big box of tissue."

Nobody had the heart to prepare Partho for what might happen, but they'd be there to deal with him if it did. This was, after all, the only family some of them had. Others had two – a biological one, in addition to their immediate dynasty forged out of necessity.

On the second night, Linnea watched Axel as he slept. Zoë stayed past her bedside shift to keep an eye on Linnea, lest she bewitch Axel in his sleep. After a couple of hours, Linnea leaned

141

in toward Axel and whispered. "What's going on in there?" She snapped her fingers to wake Zoë, who had drifted off. "Look at his eyes."

Zoë looked – beneath Axel's lids, his eyeballs were scanning rapidly back and forth. Too rapidly and too relentlessly for normal REM sleep. They gazed up at the apparatus monitoring Axel's brain waves. Whatever was happening, it was about to snap the red indicator needles right off their axis.

# Chapter 22

## Balanos

The giant oak to which Balanos was bound sprang into existence sometime in the late 1600s, though Balanos didn't come into a sense of awareness for the first 80 or 90 odd years or so – such uncommon awareness arose, in no small part, because of the village of Carnalbanagh itself, as it established itself around Balanos.

Indeed, Balanos came to believe that her consciousness and existence had been carved and framed by the villagers themselves – the villagers were so beautiful and fascinating to behold that Balanos grew to feel absolute gratitude for her small part in the extraordinarily byzantine lives of the simple folk.

Balanos was indeed a hamadryad – or wood nymph, or tree spirit, or any number of other marks that would have been meaningless to Balanos herself, which is why she did not welcome such an unnecessary and frivolous yoke.

Nor did Balanos have any particular appreciation of her prominence as daughter of Oxylus and Hamadryas, who were, after all, borne of mythology and may not ever have existed in the first place.

Balanos was, therefore, perhaps borne of mythology as well, but if anyone had asked, she would have maintained rather that she was borne of an acorn. Balanos knew that Balanos *was*, and that was certainly enough to know.

Nymphs are neither male nor female with regard to strict textbook or anatomical definition, and Balanos was no exception, though folk who believe in such things generally imagine them to be female in much the same way leprechauns are assumed to be male. Balanos therefore treasured the strengths and sympathized with the trials, tribulations and weaknesses of both earthbound sexes observed inhabiting the land beneath her sturdy branches.

Beyond the perplexing issue of the existence of at least two sexes, which Balanos alternately found intriguing and baffling, there endured a lengthy historical debate with regard to whether a wood nymph is the tree itself or the spiritual entity inhabiting said tree.

Balanos chose not to waste time with such questions whenever they attempted to demand her attention, which happened only rarely. Male or female, spirit or tree, Balanos didn't give a fig for such trivialities.

The oak tree had been a nigh on universal symbol of strength centuries before Balanos came to be. Celtic mythology, as the ancient legend would have it, considers the oak to be a "tree of doors," which serves as a gateway between worlds.

Balanos was conscious of these portals in the same way she was aware of the village and the sparrows and the sexes and the sun. The portals simply *were*, and fussing over them would never occur to Balanos, at least until such time as they proved themselves essential.

The growing season in Northern Ireland is exceedingly short, which provided Balanos with a thick, seemingly impervious bark, and an exceptionally long life. Her 200th year had come and gone without notice or fanfare nigh two score ago, and as Balanos approached what certainly might be the end of her life, the portals began to captivate her every thought.

What, exactly, *were* they? Doors to the future? Doors to the past? Passages to other dimensions and realities?

Balanos had not only developed conscious thought, she had also become curious about time and place outside the tiny village square and beyond her ken.

Balanos came to wonder if she might have options, which was an entirely new and staggering notion with enormous potential ramifications.

The question of what else, if anything, would become when she ceased to be – the moment of which Balanos innately knew must be hastily approaching – was enthralling. Balanos could not help but ponder what would come at the end and then after . . .

. . . But when the end finally did come, it did so as endings often do – quickly and unexpectedly.

Balanos typically loved the spring rains, mostly for what came next – the greening of nearby Slemish Mountain and the surrounding countryside, of which Balanos delighted in being an integral part. Balanos always took the rain to be a sign that life was about to renew itself. And indeed it was – just not in the way to which Balanos had grown accustomed.

The storm at issue blew in and engulfed the village with savage ferocity, upending both cart and cattle with indiscriminate and wild abandon. Balanos had endured her share of tempests, hundreds of them, in fact, during the two centuries and more in which she stood at the edge of the forest, eventually towering high enough to shade the village square in the afternoons when the sun was right.

This storm was different, however, for it bore fierce lightning flung powerfully, as if hurled by the angry Gods themselves.

In the end, both the strongest and weakest of the dense forest had haphazardly fallen to the storm, and still more was claimed by the ensuing fires. The sturdiest oak in all of Carnalbanagh, too, had bowed to the mightiest of the lightning bolts.

. . . But Balanos the fearlessly aware would endure – for Balanos had chosen a portal and fled with her very existence intact, just as the heavens dealt their fateful blow.

The fallen wood would be replaced by new growth in time, and perhaps even a hearty young oak would one day be gifted with the sort of awareness granted Balanos.

Or perhaps it would not. Because, after all, quite often a tree simply *is*, merely for its own sake.

# Chapter 23

## Severed Saplings

"He's awake! He's awake!" Cheryl screamed, as she galloped through the corridor and burst into the lounge where Dale, Zoë, Partho, Linnea, and Milo were trying to sleep sprawled on sofas and chairs. "Praise the good Lord above, Axel woke up!" The three days since their arrival at the intensive care unit felt like a lot longer, but Cheryl's enthusiasm quickly spread, trumping their lingering fatigue.

They waited impatiently as specialists paraded in and out of Axel's room, and then were told he was being relocated to a standard room. So they broke down their gypsy camp in the ICU lounge and emigrated to the sixth floor.

After checking on Axel, Dale called the nonresident Death Watchers while Zoë participated in a telephone conference in an effort to maintain her increasingly tenuous grasp on partnership at her firm. Cheryl and Claude went down to the car to get something sweet to steady Cheryl's nerves. Linnea, Milo, and Partho went in to see Axel, who was groggy and dazed, but happy to see them.

"I wasn't sure you'd come," he croaked to Linnea in a raspy voice.

"How could I avoid it, Axel?" Linnea grinned. "Heavens, you've got a way about you when you want a little attention."

Axel smiled at Linnea, and Partho thought he saw something pass between them. Axel turned his head toward Milo and met his gaze. "She was right, Milo – about that stupid fucking tree."

"You think so?" Milo asked sincerely, though his tone carried traces of lingering doubt.

"Right about *what?*" Partho demanded, feeling out of the loop.

Axel sighed and patted the bed to indicate that there was one hell of a story ahead if Partho had the patience for it. Partho sat down and crossed his arms testily. "*What?*"

"Apparently I'm a tree spirit. An Irish one, in fact." Axel turned to Linnea to offer clarification and inclusion. "*Northern* Ireland – a tiny village where I inhabited an oak tree until sometime in the early 1900s, I think." Axel checked Partho for a reaction before he continued, but got nothing. "Go ahead and laugh your ass off, but get it over with because I'm not going to have the patience for it later."

Partho studied Axel closely. "Nobody's laughing, Axel."

Axel looked perplexed, then shrugged. "I'm disappointed in you, Partho." After a moment, he added "At least now I know why everything overwhelms and amazes me – all those years in the tree were apparently kind of isolating."

Partho continued to search Axel's face for signs that he was being punked. "So what does this mean?"

Axel looked to Linnea, and another unspoken something passed between them; but this time Milo recognized it, too, so he provided the missing link for Partho. "I think it means Axel wants to know what he's been up to for the past century."

Linnea nodded, but in response to Axel rather than Milo. "We should do it soon."

"Do what?" Partho asked, growing impatient. He wished that they would distribute some kind of syllabus.

"We're going to hypnotize Axel and regress him into his past," Milo grinned sheepishly, almost as if he were participating in a marvelous parlor trick.

"When Axel gets well, his humanness will get in our way," Linea said, presumably for the benefit of Partho, though she remained focused on Axel. "If we're going to do this, it has to be now."

"Yes," Axel said, with a glance at Milo. "And if I don't make it . . . then at least I'll know."

"At least you'll know," Linnea agreed with such an overwhelming sense of melancholy that Partho believed, for perhaps the third or fourth time that week, that Axel might actually die.

It took half an hour to rally all hands present to Axel's bedside and insist that the medical staff leave them alone for a little while. Dale resisted, but ultimately folded under pressure from the other Death Watchers and agreed to participate. At least they were in a Beverly Hills hospital accustomed to catering to celebrities, where each and every patient bed was in a private room. Special requests, such as "Axel needs to spend a little quality time with his hypnotist and his spiritualist," didn't even raise eyebrows. Cheryl sent Claude ahead to run the shop on his own for the day because there was no frickin' way she was going to miss this.

As much as he hated to do it, Axel requested that his Dilaudid drip be removed because he didn't wish to be clouded by sedation. Dale and Zoë sat near the foot of the bed and held onto Axel's legs while Partho and Cheryl held his hands. Linnea and Milo hovered on either side, poised to whisper in Axel's ears. Axel was breathing deeply and trying to relax, though his jaw was clenched.

"Why do we have to hold onto him?" Dale asked, just as they were about to begin.

"I'm not absolutely certain," Linnea shrugged. "I think we're doing it because human contact is comforting and important." But then she quickly added an ominous codicil. "But please hang on, just in case."

"We aren't entirely sure what will happen," Milo muttered, nervously. "Maybe nothing."

Milo and Linnea knelt on either side of Axel and murmured softly into his ears. The others could feel the tension drain out of Axel's body as their gentle words urged him into a peaceful trance. Dale watched Zoë and Partho begin to sway to the gentle tempo of the words, then Cheryl joined in. After a moment, Dale even found himself connecting with their collective rhythm, his breath flowing continuously, as he surrendered to the shared reverie. Before too long, Axel began to speak . . .

$$\varnothing \quad \varnothing \quad \varnothing$$

Marcel's grandfather was among the first Frenchmen to colonize the Shanghai French Concession, expatriating to establish the settlement in 1849. Indeed in 1902, Marcel's own father helped select and plant the London Planes lined up in proud ranks on Avenue Joffre outside the large windows of the luxurious apartments he shared with his wife, Simone, their infant daughter, Odette, and several servants. The London Planes were so popular, they became known as "French Planes" to the Chinese, presumably because they had been selected and placed in neat, military rows by the occupying French.

Marcel was born a colonist, and although he was French through and through, Shanghai had always been the place he called home. With the exception of a brief interlude in Paris in order to attend University and to take a wife, it had always been Shanghai for Marcel.

Tiny Odette shivered in his arms, as he watched the wind rustle the leaves of the celebrated trees outside his window. She was no longer fussing, which should have been something of a relief, but instead felt frightening. His beloved daughter was burning with fever, her dark hair matted to Marcel's bare chest as he held her and paced his room.

Simone had been anxious about moving to what her family referred to as a "savage land," but quickly grew to adore the peaceful, civilized savages resident in the remote colony. And the help was inexpensive and plentiful too, which was important to a lady of Simone's breeding, who was accustomed to a great deal of help.

News of the Spanish Flu was slow to reach the outpost, as was the flu itself. They held out hope, in fact, that the reach of the dreaded disease would not extend to the more remote corners of the world. Such was not the case, however, and by the summer of 1919, many of the residents of the French Concession with the means to do so, spent their days fortified in their homes, preferring instead to compel their servants out on whatever household errands were absolutely required. Funeral processions, too, had become a common sight throughout all of Shanghai.

The Spanish Flu, which as it turned out, likely originated in the Far East and not in Spain at all, was the most indiscriminate virus Marcel had ever witnessed. It didn't prey necessarily on the weak, or even the elderly, the way any self-respecting virus should have done. It was just as likely to claim a vital, healthy soul, robust, and in its prime; it set about doing so in Shanghai haphazardly and with alarming regularity, triggering violent overreactions in otherwise healthy immune systems, which were often fatal.

Simone dutifully and cheerfully spent most of the summer inside, doting on little Odette, who had reached her 16th month. When Simone began showing symptoms, she immediately entrusted the care of Odette to the nanny and took to her bed, but by that time the damage was already done. She had been cuddling, entertaining, and breast feeding Odette since the beloved infant's birth, and it was reasonable to assume that whatever befell Simone might also befall dear little Odette.

As Marcel held his beautiful perfect little girl in his arms, the wee hours ticked away, and he came to understand that he would bury both a wife and a daughter before the seasons changed. Odette soon fell silent in Marcel's arms. Tiny Odette, possessed of the lively soul of a merry little elf, who entered the world amidst a violent hurricane, had departed it so very quietly. Marcel sat staring out the windows at the trees until dawn as his child grew cold in his arms.

*Odette D'Aubigne*
*April 14, 1918 – August 27, 1919*

✐   ✐   ✐

Ayako prayed for a little boy, though she felt in her heart that bringing a child into a world so fraught with war and unrest was somehow reprehensible. And of course, answered prayers are perhaps the most malicious.

Ayako had grown sick of war and the toll it was taking on all aspects of life in her village. She had hoped the relative age of her husband, Kaito, 22 years her senior, would prevent his being thrust into the fray; but after years of war, all able-bodied men were called. In the final weeks before his departure, Katio made love to his young bride with a passion and desperation generally realized only by the damned.

Such passion of course was not without consequences, and shortly after Kaito sailed away on a warship, Ayako began having morning sickness. She kept up with her job at the market and maintained her volunteer wartime duties, but grew weaker in the months leading to the delivery of her child as dread and anxiety overtook her every waking thought.

The child was born healthy and a boy, as fate would have it – to Ayako's great relief. She named him Takumi. The newborn had a light about him, and it wasn't just Ayako who could see it, as others attending the birth seemed genuinely enthralled. She could tell this was a child with determination who would grow to make her proud. She felt, just by looking at him, that nothing truly awful could ever happen again. As Ayako took Takumi into her arms, she felt truly at peace for the first time since the war began.

But Takumi wasn't the only little boy to drop from the heavens above Hiroshima that clear Monday morning, and the devastating force of the second obliterated any hopeful impact of the first. "Little Boy" was the nickname given to the gun-type fission bomb carrying 130 pounds of uranium-235, dropped by the United States Air Force – an experiment in horror and military power that would, along with its brother, nicknamed

"Fat Man," hasten the end of the war in a most devastating and unfathomable way.

Ayako believed in her final moment that the sudden flash of light surely must be heaven smiling upon her beloved son.

*Takumi Hamada*
*August 6, 1945 – August 6, 1945*

Ø   Ø   Ø

Mollie had just about had it with the arrogance, and she swore to herself that she was going to give notice after the first of the year. She didn't want to miss out on whatever holiday bonus, insufficient though it might be, that bitch Chloë might provide before she dashed off to another fab photo shoot at another groovy West End club or hurried to lunch with another too-too-marvelous boyfriend or another star-studded cocktail party, where she'd insist she was bored out of her skull.

Between fetching the special skin cream from the chemist, dropping off the chiffon at the cleaners, and delivering Chloë's regrets for some gallery opening – and oh, by the way if it's not too much trouble please dispose of that horrid infant with some charity organization that can find it a decent home – Mollie had finally reached her breaking point. She was an assistant and not a galley slave, and she certainly wasn't any sort of bloody Mary Poppins or baby merchant, either.

As far as Mollie could tell, Chloë had never held, cradled, or laid eyes on the child more than was unavoidably required, and certainly hadn't gone to the trouble of giving the wretched thing a name. Chloë was on the cusp of what would certainly be astronomical fame and fortune, after all, and an unwanted baby was more than inconvenient at a time when the brass ring was so visibly within her grasp.

Chloë had been plucked from obscurity two and a half years prior by Nigel Davies who had taken an unknown shop girl named Lesley Hornby and transformed her into an international sensation called Twiggy. And now Chloë was supposed to be next, assuming that you believed any old lie that spewed forth out of Chloë's gob, which Mollie most certainly did not. Still, Chloë had something going for her because she didn't lack for attention or dishy boyfriends. And Mollie had graciously accepted the challenge of juggling the entire circus as Chloë's assistant, secretary, and Girl Friday almost a year ago.

Chloë didn't consider the pregnancy to be anything more than a tiresome bother until she began to show, but contended that she was far too busy to take care of business then; by the time she got around to looking into that sort of business, there was nothing to be done except wait. She fled to Leeds in her fifth month, where she stayed with a discreet aunt and delivered with the aid of an equally discreet doctor; then she returned to London alone in the first class compartment, having coerced Mollie into travelling the rails in coach with the wailing infant.

The weeks since their return had been a challenge for Chloë, who seemed to have lost her place in the queue for stardom: all thanks to that insufferable child, according to Chloë. Those who eked out a living on their percent of Chloë's earnings had moved on to greener and more reliable pastures. This made Chloë's existence quite difficult and turned Mollie's life, by extension, into absolute hell.

Although she clearly had no interest in the newborn, Chloë understood that it was flesh of her flesh and blood of her blood; and as such, she believed that it certainly deserved something better than Leeds, so Mollie located a Catholic Charities hospital that housed an orphanage near central London. Not being Catholic herself or even particularly religious, Chloë decided that the best time to drop the child would be on Christmas Eve – everyone would be in a charitable mood, and perhaps so deeply entrenched in the religious fervor of the holiday that some nice people might believe it was the second coming and take the troublesome thing with them. And once they got it home and discovered that it was a baby girl rather than the Christ child, perhaps by that time the pesky details wouldn't even matter?

The foundling – and that's how Chloë always referred to the infant – *the foundling,* couldn't be abandoned by Chloë herself, of course, and couldn't be dropped off by Mollie either, lest somebody recognize her and trace the child back to Chloë. So they devised an intricate plan wherein Mollie handed the child off to a former schoolmate at a laundry shop. The friend would then place the infant in the back alley in a nondescript box, keeping an eye out until a chap on a motorbike came for it. Then he would transport it the remaining distance to the Catholics. The scheme was simple enough to accomplish and complex enough that it couldn't be easily traced; it worked brilliantly, at least up to a point.

The bloke on the motorbike felt awkward dropping the child near the front door because so many people were hurrying in and out with gifts and food and holiday whatnot, so he instead left the baby on the less travelled backstairs near the door to the kitchen. Someone would come across it before very long and bring it inside, especially once it started to cry, so he pulled his jacket tighter against the cold and hurried home in the freezing rain to his own family who were waiting to raise their Christmas cheer.

*Frozen Baby Doe*
*November 28, 1969 – December 25, 1969*

✄   ✄   ✄

A xel woke up agitated, distressed, and gasping for breath. "Oh my God! I'm no fucking good at any of this! No fucking good at all!" He looked at the astonished faces surrounding him, and despite his grief and rage, he almost laughed – he'd never seen quite so many familiar faces so utterly flabbergasted at exactly the same time.

*"Axel!"* Cheryl cried, completely in awe and with her lip quivering. "Honey, you're *excellent* at this! Land sakes, if anybody back home in Eagle Harbor could reach all the way back like you do, the Yoopers'd never stop gossipin' about it!"

"Oh my God!" Axel wailed. "I can't even survive *infancy*, for fuck's sake!"

They let Axel rant for several minutes before he grew tired and fell quiet. When he did, it was Linnea who spoke first. "You know, there's one more, Axel."

"What if it's not any better?"

"Then at least you'll know," Milo interjected, somewhat nervously.

"Fuck you, Milo!" Axel growled.

"We'll have to deepen your trance. You're resisting, for some reason."

"I'm way ahead of you," Axel murmured, inhaling deeply and inducing his muscles to relax. "With my run of luck I was probably the fucking *Lindberg Baby.*"

Linnea nodded to the others who each took hold of Axel with both hands, which in the end turned out to be a very good thing.

☙ ☙ ☙

The sunny blonde child was born to the outdoors, delighting in the ducklings and the chickens and the mud and the bugs. His self-sufficient nature was a relief to both his parents, who already had a houseful, in addition to the ongoing demands of the land. He was content to play with his brothers or the neighbor children, or the animals themselves, who all seemed to take a shine to the boy.

Occasionally, his curious nature would get the better of him and he would follow one of the piglets into the barn or hide in the hay or other such nonsense; but his antics were no worse than any of the other boys, and his sweet nature and soulful blue eyes bailed him out of most of the hot water he managed to get himself into. His mother particularly found disciplining the child more difficult than with the others because she was reaching the end of her childbearing years and he would, therefore, always be her baby.

But life on the farm was difficult and demanding, and no one could be expected to keep an eye on him every single minute. That's what the entire community said in the days and weeks that followed the terrible disaster in order to console his mother, as well as themselves. Bad things sometimes happen to good people; and when they do it's just God's way, and there's nothing to be done but persevere stoically onward.

Three days after his ill-fated encounter with the thresher, the larger, arguably identifiable chunks of Axel Hooley were buried adjacent to the farmhouse where Isaac and Annie Hooley hosted church services in their basement the third Sunday every other month. The Hooleys, like the larger community around them, were a devout, modest folk, preferring to deal with private matters in the traditional Amish ways.

Annie Hooley remained thereafter, inconsolable.

*Axel Hooley*
*February 20, 1977 – July 17, 1979*

🐚 🐚 🐚

The discreet indirect designer lighting began to flicker all over the sixth floor, and most assumed that it was the emergency generators kicking on in response to an unexpected, though not entirely uncommon Southern California brownout. Those within view of room 623, however, were given an entirely different impression altogether – lightning flashed from beneath the door and water gushed out of the cracks in the doorjamb. A woman on the street below reported seeing a tree burst out the window with branches spiraling upwards.

"Don't let go!" Linnea screamed to the others, as they soared erratically above the patchwork of corn and wheat fields and grain silos and herds of terrified dairy cows. Linnea held tight around Milo and clenched Axel's right arm precariously while Cheryl dangled from his left, shrieking.

Partho had managed to wrap his legs up around Axel's torso and was arched backward with one arm extended, holding onto Zoë, who linked precariously between Partho's grasp and Axel's left leg. Dale dangled from Axel's right foot, holding on with all his might using both hands. Zoë believed that Dale and Milo had both most likely gone into shock.

If the scenery gusting past was any indication, they hovered somewhere over the Midwest and at the mercy of a spinning, angry tornado that had erupted from deep within Axel once he discovered the truth. Whatever Linnea had tried to prepare them for, this certainly wasn't it; and she was as surprised as anyone. Lightning flashed around them, though the real terror stemmed from the idea that Axel might shake one of them off with his bucking and thrashing. If that happened, she wasn't at all certain what might become of the unfortunate soul. Linnea couldn't tell for sure if they were really over the Midwest or suspended somewhere between the earthly dimension and the next.

Linnea knew she had to reach Axel, but to do so, she was going to have to climb over Milo. So she kicked off her pumps and began crawling her way up Milo's back, glancing down only once to bid farewell and safe travels to her shoes.

"*Ow!*" Milo shouted as she reached his shoulder. "What are you—?"

"I have to reach Axel," she screamed above the squall, grateful that Milo was still intellectually linked up.

Linnea clawed her way up Axel's hospital gown and clasped both hands around his neck, dragging herself close to his ear.

"*You are Axel Hooley!*" She screamed. "*You are Axel Hooley and by God this will not finish you!*"

Axel began lashing violently, and Linnea could hear the wails of her fellow travelers as they struggled to hold on. She pulled him closer. "*You belong with us and we will not let you go!! Not ever! You are alive and you are loved and you . . . are . . . not . . . done!*"

Partho glanced up and saw Linnea do the most primitive beast-like thing he'd ever seen an elegant, well-mannered, civilized lady do – she opened her mouth and bit down hard on Axel's ear.

That seemed to do the trick because the next thing they knew, they were all plummeting from the sky toward what none of them could imagine would be anything but a certain quick and violent death.

∅ ∅ ∅

When the door to room 623 burst open, a tidal wave of water, terrified Death Watchers, and tree branches flooded into the hallway. Maintenance workers cleaning up the mess later also found two dead chickens, a weathervane, and more than a dozen stalks of corn.

The hospital administrator who called the authorities in to investigate was quickly collared by Zoë, who filed an official complaint regarding the broken water pipe and faulty electrical wiring in Axel's room and promised swift and robust legal action if things weren't immediately rectified to her satisfaction. She suggested that, assuming that her friend didn't die from the obvious maintenance neglect, they might overlook the pain and suffering incurred in the tragic mishap if Cedars-Sinai saw fit to waive Axel's current and mounting hospital expenses. If not, she had friends at the local NBC affiliate, and it wouldn't take more than a phone call to have the story on the news that night.

Axel was quickly cleaned up, thoroughly checked over, and moved to one of the lavish hospital suites generally reserved for celebrity patients.

As Axel drifted in and out of consciousness that evening, several Death Watchers heard him mumble "I'm Axel Hooley. I'm really, *really* Axel Hooley." There was some discussion about whether he felt good about that or not.

Linnea was sitting with him, still holding onto his hand when his eyes opened with the inquisitive gaze of a child. "I'm really him? I'm Axel Hooley?"

"Yes Axel, you are," Linnea nodded reassuringly. "A couple of times."

# Chapter 24

# The Ivy

Axel opened his eyes and gazed up at Linnea, startled by how sunny it was in the front room of her Culver City bungalow. She'd been trying to put him under and he wasn't certain exactly how long he'd been lying there in pursuit of a hypnotic trance.

"I don't think it's going to work. All I can think about is lunch."

Linnea smiled and nodded. "I suspected as much. You're getting your strength back – your brute, animal strength. Which is excellent news, of course, from a strictly human standpoint."

"But what about all the other stuff?" Axel asked warily. "I mean, where did it all go?" He was four months out of treatment and still looked peaked and frail. Axel hoped to unravel one last mystery before Balanos burrowed her way back into his deep psyche, taking his biggest secret with her.

"Your spirit is as strong as ever, Axel – stronger, probably, because now you've been challenged." Linnea patted his leg to signal him that they were finished and he could sit up.

Axel sat up from the chaise. He looked down at his body, which was still rail thin, despite his regaining 20 or so of the 60 pounds he'd lost during his ordeal. He rubbed his eyes and stretched. "It would be nice if I could get an image or part of a name – anything."

"I understand," Linnea smiled sadly. "But you probably know too much already. You have more information about your origins than just about anybody – is it really so essential to find out who provided the genetic material that made you?"

"I'd still like to know—"

Linnea cut him off rather than indulge his floundering. "Anything that you are, hereditarily or genetically, Axel, is of the least possible importance. I know that for sure. It's fleeting, and more temporary than any other part of you."

"How can I be sure any of my past lives are real? The more time that passes, the more everything seems like something I dreamt up or fantasized."

Linnea shook her head. "I don't think so, Axel. People fantasize they were Cleopatra or King Arthur or Napoleon, when in fact we were most often eunuchs and sharecroppers and peasants. If you were fantasizing, I think you'd come up with something a bit more exotic than four children cut down before they got on their feet."

Axel nodded his reluctant agreement. "I only got answers to questions I didn't even know I had."

"It's okay to ponder and speculate. You're like a racehorse who's had trouble clearing the paddock – you're so thrilled to be off your tether, you go wild and bump around and fall down and want answers, answers, answers. But if you fall wrong, you'll break your leg and then I'm going to be the one who has to shoot you. It's time to start moving forward again." Linnea went into the kitchen and returned a moment later with two glasses of lemonade. "Stay hydrated. I can't believe you rode here on your bicycle."

Axel smiled. "I'm trying to build my strength, so I don't drive unless I have to. I keel over every two or three blocks and gasp for air a lot, but I think it's good for me. I'm meeting Sylvia and Esperanza for lunch at The Ivy. They'll give me a ride home."

"With your bicycle?"

"I put a bike rack on the back of Sylvia's Beemer," he grinned.

"How's it going? With Sylvia, I mean?"

"It's alright," Axel shrugged. A month after he finished treatment, his landlady moved into a senior care facility, so Axel carted his few belongings from his above-garage apartment at Aunt Bea's to Sylvia's guest house. "I was only going to stay a month or so, you know – clean the pool, do a few handyman chores, maybe paint a couple rooms . . ." Axel drifted off.

"What?" Linnea asked, sensing he was holding something back.

"I don't think I'm really there to upgrade the bathroom and clean the pool."

Linnea nodded and understood.

"Sylvia's 94," Axel said abruptly, as if the news in itself was heartbreaking. "Esperanza told me – neither of them can keep a secret worth a damn. Sylvia will admit to being in her late 70s, but that's as high as she goes, officially. She needs someone there besides Esperanza, and I need someplace to be."

"I think that's nice," Linnea smiled. "And your other friends? Back to normal?"

Axel grinned. "If *normal* is what you want to call them, then yeah. Tyrell roped Cheryl and Claude into volunteering with his youth ministry, so now they have teenage street kids to fuss over instead of me. Cheryl always smells like weed, so they *completely* trust her. Maude's helping a few of the kids with college applications, too. So I guess hooking everybody up turned out to be a good thing."

"Of course it was," Linnea frowned, wondering how Axel could ever have believed it would be otherwise.

"The most random things draw people together, and you never can tell if the mix is going to turn into a tasty salad or a nuclear meltdown." Axel chuckled, pleased with his analogy. "And Rhymey keeps asking Zoë to marry him, which is totally great and maybe even perfect, so of course Zoë keeps trying to dump him. Rhymey can be relentless when he wants something though, so they'll probably end up married – at least for a little while. And Dale's cats are back home, but he's changed their names from "The Captain and Tennille" to *Odette* and *Takumi*.

Linnea brayed that wonderful laugh and nearly spat out a mouthful of lemonade. "You must be so very honored."

"Oh, I am," Axel assured her. "Zoë nicknamed her breasts the same thing, which is an even *better* honor."

Linnea shrugged, as if everybody had such idiosyncrasies. "Mine are named *Maddy* and *Moe*."

"A couple of my massage clients want me back whenever I'm ready to work again. But I'm only going to be giving legit massages from here on out."

"Meaning?" Linnea asked, though Axel couldn't tell if she was joking or not.

Axel blushed slightly. "Meaning . . . people need to take responsibility for their own happy endings."

They sat for a few minutes gazing through the window screens out into the street. Axel tolerated the extended silence well enough, which spoke volumes with regard to how safe he still felt with Linnea. He was a little sad at having lost the intense spiritual connection they'd shared, but of course anything so powerful was ultimately going to have a limited shelf life. Finally, he spoke. "Where do I go? When I'm not here, I mean – when I'm not Axel Hooley or one of the others who didn't survive? Where do you think I go I when I'm not here?" Axel pressed down his palms, which Linnea correctly took to mean *earthbound*.

Linnea furrowed her brow for a moment, aware that Axel couldn't endure another sustained silence. Still, she didn't speak.

"There are gaps, you know – *huge* gaps," Axel continued. "Where was I in the 1920s and 1930s? What happened to me between the bombing of Hirosima and that shitty Christmas in London?"

"You have to understand that time as we know it only happens in a linear fashion in the here and now. Other dimensions are more compact or more expansive or nonlinear. Maybe you go from one existence straight into the next? Or maybe you go wherever you went when you very nearly died, right before that last trip to the hospital?"

"You really don't know, do you?" Axel asked dryly, making it obvious that he wasn't at all surprised.

Linnea responded with a "Nope" that sounded so definitive it felt almost as if it were the thorough explanation he was seeking.

Axel's voice caught as he spoke. "I just don't think I ever want to be a tree again. Trees are nice and all, but . . ."

Linnea smiled. "I think a tree spirit has to very badly want to become something else in order to accomplish it. I can't imagine there's any going back."

"Do you mind if I ask you a favor?" Axel asked softly. "It's kind of personal."

Linnea felt suddenly awkward, but shrugged and nodded.

"I've got these three pin-point tattoos they gave me in radiology so they could triangulate and focus my radiation." Axel lifted his shirt to point out two tiny points on each of his sides and one on his belly.

"They're very tiny," Linnea said. "I wouldn't have noticed them."

"Well, as long as they're there, I want to do something with them."

"What kind of something?"

"I want to incorporate them into a tattoo, I think – something to memorialize the whole experience – my cancer, my four dead babies, my friends – all of it. Is that gruesome?"

"I don't think it's gruesome at all, Axel. I think it's kind of nice."

"Anyway, a wood nymph would look really gay. I'd need three of them, which is excessively gay and wouldn't even make sense because I'd feel like I also needed a fourth one somewhere to commemorate Axel the first, and that just seems ultra gay, even for my taste. The only unifying thing I can come up with is an oak tree, but that's also problematic and probably a little weird even for a tattoo. So I was thinking maybe some kind of foliage might do the trick?"

"Foliage?" Linnea asked, crinkling her brow, then finishing up with a bright smile.

"Not *shrubbery* for fuck's sake," Axel said, with a laugh. "Maybe some kind of vine or branch or ivy or something that would wrap around and incorporate all three points? Nobody would really know what it meant of course, but *we* would know."

"That sounds beautiful, Axel," Linnea said.

"I thought, maybe, if you didn't mind . . ."

"What are you getting at?" she demanded. "Spit it out."

"I was hoping you would let me take a picture of your tattoo – the winding floral vine pattern on your upper arm. I wouldn't totally rip off your design or anything – just something I could use to explain the kind of thing I want."

Linnea seemed genuinely touched. "Of course, Axel. You won't need a picture, though – whenever you're ready, I'll take you to my tattoo artist and he can design artwork similar to mine."

Axel raised his eyebrows. "You have a tattoo guy?"

Linnea nodded. "Renny. He's a very good tattoo guy, in fact – gentle, spiritual – one of the oldest souls you'll ever meet."

"An old soul, huh?" Axel sighed, wistfully.

"Yes, Axel – you're a zygote by comparison."

Axel nodded. "You're great, Linnea. Thanks." He picked up his bicycle helmet and made his way toward the door as Linnea followed. "There's one more important thing."

"What's that?"

Axel turned and confronted Linnea determinedly. "You need to give Milo a chance."

"Milo?" Linnea grinned. "Milo's very sweet, but he must be a dozen, maybe fifteen years younger than I—"

"I don't give a damn," Axel insisted. There was clarity in his voice, despite his obvious discomfort raising the subject. "Milo's great, and as it turns out he was right about everything – knowing *is* better. Whenever I sort out exactly what it is I know, I'm going to want Milo to help me figure out what it all means."

"Ha!" Linnea guffawed, which, in turn, made Axel laugh. "Good heavens, Axel, nobody has a clue what it all means." They both knew that Linnea was trying to weasel out of having the Milo discussion, but she still wanted to make her point. "We won't know what our current lives are about until much later."

"Okay, Linnea," Axel held her gaze. "If that's the case, what are my *past* lives about? Why bother being born just to have the rug jerked out from under me before I ever got a decent shot?"

Linnea was careful with her words. "Even if we only exist briefly, that moment can trigger other moments that affect people and things and souls and lives – things we're too simple and human to understand. Our job is just to be."

"*To be?*" he asked, incredulously. "Hmm . . . '*To be or not to be?*'" A frown creased Axel's forehead in an expression that managed to similarly reflect one of Linnea's. "That's astoundingly irritating and not at all helpful."

Linnea looked perplexed for a moment as she thought about it. "In that case, just try to be nice to people." After a moment, she continued slowly but with conviction. "And give generously to charity and be gentle with the earth and respectful to animals." She finished up with a shrug. "And a daily exercise regimen augmented with a decent multivitamin supplement won't kill you, either."

"Okay," Axel shrugged. The last of their otherworldly connection had dribbled away and surrendered to homilies and sage advice.

"You're still very young, Axel Hooley, but please don't forget that you were once a very *old* tree. That counts for a lot."

"I guess that'll have to be enough," Axel smiled. And Linnea could tell that it was, at least for now. "Now do us all a favor and give Milo a fucking telephone call."

🌣  🌣  🌣

Axel was not a great fan of The Ivy, generally speaking, particularly the patio where Sylvia preferred to dine with the paparazzi peeking at them over the hedge. Though Axel wasn't their target, he still felt as if the world was just waiting for him to catch some spinach in his teeth or pick his nose. The front patio could just as easily be star-studded as it could be populated with Hollywood poser-pixies who were there to nibble their watercress and sparkle for the cameras. The food was always adequate, if a little pricey; but it wasn't his money, so if Sylvia wanted to pay for atmosphere, atmosphere is what she'd get.

He waved at Sylvia and Esperanza on his way to the bathroom, which he always did first thing upon arriving at The Ivy to make sure that he was handsome and well-groomed enough for the room. Today he looked sallow and sweaty, but even that was a recent improvement. He kissed both Sylvia and Esperanza on the cheek in a debonair Cary Grant fashion as he sat down at the table.

"I just saw Ewan McGregor come out of the restroom."

"Yes, Axel," Sylvia muttered, distractedly as she scanned the list of specials through her trifocals. "Everybody poops."

"You keep an eye on the ol' lady while I do my shopping," Esperanza demanded as soon as he sat down. "Dowager's a pain en mí cola."

"Go ahead, doll, have fun." Sylvia forced a toothy smile on Esperanza and looked for a moment as if she were posing for a black and white photo spread in an old *Life* magazine. "I only keep you around in case I find myself unexpectedly floundering in the Rio Grande."

Once Esperanza made her getaway, Sylvia patted Axel's arm and leaned in to whisper quietly. "Get anything you want – my treat."

"Of course it's your treat, Sylvia," Axel teased. "I don't have any money."

"Not to worry, dear – when you've got good friends, you're rich."

"Oh? Then what are you if you have rich friends?"

"*Selective!*" Sylvia barked, gleefully. She was in a rare mood and completely in her element. Axel couldn't imagine that The Ivy had been conceived with anybody but Sylvia in mind.

Axel scanned the menu to find whatever offered the most protein. Now that his body had stopped burning lean tissue, he wanted to try to put the weight back on in more or less the same places from whence it departed. He needed to have a serious conversation with Sylvia, and doing it while they were distracted by menus, people watching, and stargazing would be ideal.

"I'm thinking of going away for a little while." He glanced at Sylvia to gauge her reaction, which was as predicted, imperceptible.

Sylvia's silence roared around Axel like a typhoon, but he sat quietly and allowed it to occur without interrupting. When Sylvia did speak, her tone was as dry as a bone. "Have we somehow managed to offend you?"

"Of course not. Everyone has been more than amazing. But I've been a burden for a long time now, and I should probably give all of you a break." There was another silence, but Axel couldn't bear this one. "And maybe I can give myself a little break, too."

"What exactly do you consider to be a 'break?'" Sylvia asked, closing her menu and looking up for the first time.

"I haven't thought it through specifically. And I can't say that I would be gone long, necessarily. But I also couldn't say when I'd be coming back . . . necessarily. I just want to find some way to move ahead."

"Move ahead? There's not much point in moving if you're not going *toward* something."

"Like I said, I don't know for sure. I might try to find a more spiritual place, maybe? Do a little time at a monastery or something? Maybe go someplace where I can figure out what I'm supposed to do and where I'm supposed to do it."

"I thought you made your voyage of self-discovery already? Aren't you some kind of nutty leprechaun or something?" Axel had become an expert at recognizing the merry dance in Sylvia's eyes, whether they were actually focused on him or not.

"This isn't a question of who I am – I'm getting a pretty good handle on that, oddly enough." Axel took Sylvia's hand to keep her attention. "This is about my life having some sort of point."

"If you have some idea who you are, doll, you're way ahead of most people."

"That's probably true," Axel agreed.

"But I don't see any purpose in going off like some philosophical loose cannon, as if you're some modern-day Khalil Gibran."

Axel had recently won a few rounds with Sylvia, so now she liberally and unfairly dispensed references she knew he wouldn't understand – and it worked as planned because she was back on top. After all, Sylvia had logged more time in her one life than he had in his entire human catalog.

"If you're looking for a spiritual place, Axel, you should look inside first." Sylvia pointed to her chest and then to Axel before patting his shrunken pecs with the palm of her hand. "And there's no better place for introspection than right here in Beverly Hills."

"You know, Sylvia – some say we're a little shallow and self-centered out here." Axel insisted.

"Why would anyone deliberately leave Beverly Hills? We're not without our eccentricities of course, but it's ideal for you, spiritually or otherwise. Don't even try to deny it. I know best."

Axel shrugged in vague agreement, realizing that she wasn't going to drop it.

"We have our own city hall, our own library, our own police and fire department, and our own tax base. Beverly Hills is an oasis amid the madness. You're not going to find another place like it; I can promise you that."

"What about West Hollywood?" The trigger in Axel's brain went off, warning him about the futility of going head to head with Sylvia, but he ignored it. "It's independently incorporated and has all its own services and city hall and crap."

"Yes, West Hollywood is an oasis of sorts – if you're *gay*." Sylvia looked stunned for a moment, as if she'd never considered the possibility. "*Are* you gay?"

Axel shrugged as an eavesdropping paparazzi snapped his photo in case he was a celebrity on the cusp of a sexual epiphany. "It depends on who you talk to. I've tried it, but it didn't work any better than anything else, and it was a total failure in lots of ways that I suspect are probably important."

"It doesn't matter," Sylvia shrugged, indifferent. "I just like knowing things."

"I'm keeping my options open," Axel sighed.

"My point is," Sylvia continued, refusing to be distracted. "Beverly Hills is perfect – completely self-sustaining and as spiritual as anybody ever needs to be. We're practically the Vatican."

Axel laughed in spite of himself and choked on his water. It took him a moment to realize he'd heard the words before – *said* them, in fact, months earlier, while sprawled out on a lawn in his underpants trying to sort out his identity. The words that reached him that day were Sylvia's, though she hadn't yet given voice to them. Axel didn't know what it was supposed to mean, but it confirmed what he already knew – they were connected – all of them. And whether he understood the connections or not, they were there, and there they would remain.

In addition, there was something hilarious about this Jewish woman who was closing in on the end of a century, waxing poetic about Beverly Hills and the human spirit, and then driving her point home with a sentimental reference to the historic hotbed of Catholicism – and to top it off, the whole thing made some kind of reasonable sense. The repercussions of Sylvia's remark harkened back through time, not only to Axel months before, but down through the ages, integrating centuries of culture shuffling, mixing and matching of ethnicity and belief to a point where the two of them, dissimilar as they were, could dine comfortably in an overpriced restaurant pretending that they were celebrities and discussing whether they were spiritual enough. It implied that, despite the strife-riddled conflicted world they had to find a way to inhabit, at least some semblance of spiritual awareness was manifesting itself in gentle ways at Axel's table.

"Sylvia," Axel said, unsure how he was going to unravel his thoughts. "I may have to live 100 lifetimes before I understand things as clearly as you do."

He sat there holding onto Sylvia's hand for a long moment, enjoying the sun peeking through the trees. The Ivy was busy, and he felt they should hurry up and order so that they could eat and surrender the table to one of the predatory parties hovering impatiently at the entrance. Sylvia had apparently drifted into her afternoon nap a little early, however, so Axel waved the waiter away when he arrived.

Then in one shocking instant, Axel realized that Sylvia was gone. Not completely gone – not yet, anyway, but certainly ready for liftoff. Panic welled up inside him and he froze, despite his every impulse imploring him to leap up and call for help, to pull Sylvia from her chair and pound on her chest – to breathe life into her from his own lungs for as long as his depleted body could manage. But something in the feel of Sylvia's hand cautioned him against such action. He sat, paralyzed with fear and overwhelmed by the immensity of what was about to transpire. He took a deep breath and leaned in close to Sylvia, still holding onto her hand, with tears flooding down his face. He whispered quietly through his clenched jaw. "Okay, Sylvia – if that's *really* what you want – I'll wait."

He felt a tug on Sylvia's hand, but understood that it wasn't Sylvia's doing – it was as if someone had taken hold of her free hand and gently pulled her through to the other side. Axel didn't have any idea who it was, but he was very grateful that someone Sylvia loved had come for her.

It was such a quiet thing.

Axel glanced around the restaurant and realized that he was the only one there who had felt anything magnificent or out of the ordinary. Even the paparazzi were engrossed with inconsequential afternoon things, just as if it were a regular day in Beverly Hills.

The tug on Sylvia's hand was the last undeniable connection he felt to his immortal self – to Balanos – that he felt for a long while. There were moments when Axel had his suspicions, of course, but most of the time he was too caught up in being human to know for sure.

He sat there wondering what Sylvia would want him to do next. She certainly deserved better than to have the paparazzi and celebrity wannabes gawking at her stiffening carcass, but he hadn't a clue how to spirit her out of there without causing some kind of a fuss.

Axel ultimately decided Sylvia hadn't chosen The Ivy by accident – there was only one reason to go to The Ivy, after all – and that was because you *wanted* a fuss.

So that's exactly the sort of gargantuan, over-the-top, cluster-fuck sendoff Axel gave her.

𝄢 𝄢 𝄢

Linnea thought about Axel all afternoon, though she was confident she had done the right thing. It was all but impossible to hypnotize a hungry person in a sunlit room – fortunately Axel didn't know that.

The experience in Axel's hospital room had been as much of a shock for Linnea as it was for Axel, and once she saw the whole picture, she did what she had to in order to shield him. If Axel had comprehended the whole unvarnished truth, he might have blown to pieces high above an Indiana cornfield somewhere in the next dimension, taking his fellow voyagers along with him.

Axel's questions about his current mortal lineage were the only ones remaining; and without some mystery, Linnea was afraid he might lose the spark driving him to form strong connections – without connections, Axel would certainly be lost. Linnea didn't want to be responsible for losing him. Not again.

She knew that she had to spin Axel around and point him toward the future, especially after such an intense look back – it was the least any good mother could do. She would tell him the truth one day – she promised herself that she would. But not just yet. Knowing would only make him feel betrayed right now. Besides, once she grew closer to the blood and bones Axel Hooley inhabiting planet Earth in the twenty-first century, she could begin thinking about revealing herself.

Linnea hadn't intentionally abandoned her child, of course. She loved her enchanting little boy, despite his peculiarities. She blamed his odd ethereal manner on her own erratic behavior – she spent her late teen years and beyond absorbed by angry predictable rebellion against the entitlements lavished on her and the rules imposed by her callous father and alcoholic mother on Chicago's affluent Gold Coast. Her efforts to find her own brand of uniqueness led her to New York, where she became unique in exactly the same ways as everybody else who ever fled one leviathan metropolis for another.

Linnea's pregnancy was unexpected, though not unwelcome; and the boy was named Sergio after his father, a Peruvian bass player who she thought she might have loved, though he died from a heroin overdose four months before his son's birth.

"Axel" was a much better moniker than "Sergio," and Linnea wondered why she hadn't come up with it in the first place. No matter how it's spelled, an axle is a hub to which dozens of spokes connect, and that felt right in so many ways – so much better than honoring the semi-talented, self-destructive, drug-addicted father he never knew. Linnea wasn't as spiritually hooked up in her earlier years, so she forgave herself for the oversight and thanked the fates for adjusting the gears as they did.

After years of wandering from one fad, religion, job, and bed to the next, Linnea reached a point where she knew she couldn't remain in the city because the madness she'd conjured up there was starting to filter into her son. So she agreed to return home to Chicago, where her hypercritical parents could care for her and spend their declining years in constant disapproval of her bastard child. That is assuming of course they would even consent to acknowledge the boy once she showed up with him bundled in her arms.

She had only pulled the rental car over so that she could go to the restroom and pick up some fresh fruit for dinner at one of the roadside farm stands. Sergio was never a child who enjoyed staying put, but she was only away for a few minutes. She became frantic in her efforts to find him, pushing her way through the masses at the harvest festival, where she correctly assumed that he had wandered.

By the time she found him, he was cradled in the desperate embrace of a weeping woman in peculiar *Little House on the Prairie* garb surrounded by her family and closely safeguarded by robust, bearded pioneer men. When the child met her gaze, Linnea saw that something within him deeply needed to stay. She had long considered that moment – that psychic flash – to be the one that opened her up to an entire world of new experiences. Sergio didn't run crying into her open arms, after all, and his eyes told her undeniably that he was where he was supposed to be. Now she understood – some missed experience needed to be accumulated, and Linnea could not be the one to provide it.

Linnea stayed in the area for more than a week, fretting over whether she was doing the right thing. Who was more gentle, caring, and grounded than the Amish, after all? The air was clean, the food was fresh, and the people were goodhearted and the salt of the earth. Sergio would be safe here. And what's more, he wouldn't have to endure the constant judgment and rejection in the only home Linnea was able to provide.

Linnea experienced the first of many visions that week in her seedy hotel. The wall of her room seemingly dissolved into two pathways – one where she and her son travelled together which felt most definitely as if it were not destined to be followed. The other path split and wound haphazardly through unfamiliar countryside, where she and her son each travelled alone. While Linnea was apprehensive and fearful of the chaotic and dangerous path, she understood that it was the one she must choose, and also saw that they would one day reconnect.

In the end, Linnea drove off alone. She reported Sergio missing when she arrived in Chicago, so Chicago is where the authorities looked, though she knew he would never be found anywhere near One Mag Mile. She never spoke with her parents about her son, and spent less than a month in Chicago before getting back into her car and heading west, which was the only decision up to that point that she never questioned.

Linnea fully intended to go back for him when the time was right – once his character became grounded and stable – perhaps then he might be in need of, or impervious to, the disorder that life with his mother would provide.

She went back to Amish Acres every year for the harvest festival and purchased strawberries from him at a farm stand on occasion. She even bought him a ticket to see a movie once when she spotted him hustling tourists outside a Cineplex. She followed him in and sat three rows behind, observing quietly. It occurred to her later that she hadn't followed the feature at all, but watching her little boy for 90 uninterrupted minutes had been magical. But mostly Linnea kept her distance.

She hadn't known, of course, that Amish boys come of age at 16, nor was she aware that he had been anointed with the identity of a deceased child nearly three years his senior. She also didn't understand how anybody could find the boy to be anything but delightful, or how truly loving people could ever let him go – but of course, she was in no position to pass judgment. Once she discovered that he was gone, she understood it was for good; she had no choice but to place her trust in the clarity of her visions.

Years later, she hired a private investigator to find him, but the only thing he turned up was a stripper in Las Vegas who may or may not be gay. She certainly couldn't imagine any kind of plausible course of events in which *that* jarring transition could ever have come about. So she let it go and held tightly to her belief that he would return when the time was right.

Linnea was of the belief that lives could go horribly off-track if the puzzle pieces fit together too cleanly – she had seen it happen. She believed that the desperate human struggle to complete the picture was perhaps the one true key to the joy of living. And she most certainly wanted bountiful, abundant, overwhelming, and plenteous joy for Axel. Linnea wondered if she would be able to maintain her own lust for life now that her puzzle had come together so perfectly.

She picked up the phone to call Milo – maybe he was in the mood for dinner and a stunning confession? She had no reason to believe that she and Milo had any sort of romantic future together, but she thought she might very much enjoy knocking his socks off.

Axel would be back; she was sure of that much. And maybe then she would tell him the rest of his story. And hers. Or maybe she would wait. In the meantime, Axel would have her tattoos.

# Chapter 25

# Evergreen

℘  ℘  ℘

The *Beverly Hills Courier* carried alongside the notice of Sylvia's death a number of unflattering photographs of some rather shaken celebrities, which were picked up by the tabloids and widely distributed.

Zoë and Dale helped select a new suit for Axel because they all agreed that Sylvia would want him to attend her funeral looking as much like a gigolo as possible.

The house went to Esperanza Baum with the non-binding-but-understood caveat that Axel Hooley could stay – and Axel Hooley could stay with the non-binding-but-understood caveat that he would keep the pool clean. Axel was also included in Sylvia's Will at the same inheritance rank as her nieces and nephews.

While it didn't make him rich, Axel was able to reimburse Zoë and Dale for part of the colossal expense they fronted in order to save his life; more specifically, to save it in Beverly Hills. The money that remained allowed him a little breathing room, so he took the opportunity to go up into the mountains and actually breathe.

🖋 🖋 🖋

The pair had to stop every so often on their way up the trail so that Axel could rest, but Partho didn't seem to mind.

Axel had hugged Zoë and Rhymey goodbye down at the Valley Forge trailhead, where they would wait for Partho who was to accompany Axel up to the ridge.

Dale said his goodbyes earlier in the day, right after breakfast, and the remaining Death Watchers said their farewells over dinner the night before. Dale was seeing someone new – an architect with whom Axel was not involved in selecting for him, which was probably for the best. Axel promised Dale he would try not to kill this one off, at least for a while.

Goodbyes were awkward for Axel, and Partho's was going to be the most difficult because he suspected Partho might not understand that even a big goodbye wasn't necessarily forever. Axel had come to believe, in fact, that no goodbye could actually ever *be* forever.

They hiked up through the evergreens mostly in silence, and kept looking back at the sweeping view of the Los Angeles basin. The autumn day was so crisp and clear that they could see the Pacific Ocean glittering in the distance.

Axel's strength was ebbing back, though not nearly as quickly as he wanted it. His body chemistry had also changed – he now required eight hours sleep instead of the formerly requisite six. And his hair and fingernails had begun to grow out again, though his hair was coming in white now with only a singular patch of his formerly dark color on the right side. He wondered if his change in follicle pigment was due to the chemo or getting older or what? He suspected it was because of the volume of physical and emotional trauma he'd accumulated. His fingernails and toenails still sported ugly yellow ridges where the chemotherapy had halted his cell reproduction for a time, but he expected that they would grow out in a month or two.

And now he woke up every day with an intense and essential need to stay connected and make the most of every experience that came his way. Axel was afraid that might fade with time, but he intended to do his damnedest to hang onto it for as long as possible.

In the end, Axel listened to his heart rather than to Sylvia, despite her last words about staying put in Beverly Hills, which would continue to gnaw at him. If he went away for a little while, perhaps it would enable him to feel right about coming back. Besides, it was a big world, and as long as he wasn't rooted into the earth, he wanted to go experience it.

He could have flown (commercially, of course), but that would demand more specificity and decision making than Axel was willing to muster. Leaving town on foot gave him more options. Hiking over Mount Wilson and coming out the other side was as far ahead as he had planned. He would go north or east from there and maybe even catch a ride with someone new who was pointed in whichever direction his heart pulled him.

As they approached the summit, they stopped and sat down on a fallen pine log. Axel looked out over Los Angeles and pondered exactly how he should approach the next few minutes. Before he could synthesize anything practical, Partho chimed in.

"So where will you go, Axel? What do you think you will do?"

"I don't know," he admitted. "But I'm pretty sure it's completely normal to not know what's ahead."

Axel gazed out over L.A. and silently thanked the beautiful city for coughing up the persons and resources required to spare him for this moment. Though his departure was imminent, neither he nor Partho were quite ready, so Axel waited for another cue.

"I don't understand what happened to all of us that day in your hospital room."

Axel heaved an amused sigh. "Well, Parth, I think—"

"Don't try to explain it!" Partho insisted, cupping his hands over his ears. "You only complicate everything when you talk. I'll decide for myself what it means."

Axel nodded and grinned. "That's probably for the best."

Partho followed Axel's gaze out over their gorgeous city. "Who knew it was so beautiful?"

"Yeah," Axel agreed, trying to memorize the moment, complete with the accompanying breathtaking view. "What do you mean, I 'complicate everything?'"

"You need to think things out thoroughly in your head first," Partho said. "It will make you seem less crazy. Everybody runs for cover when you open your mouth and start sorting your laundry."

Axel nodded and smiled. "Point taken." Each passing moment was becoming more difficult.

"You're coming back for my graduation?"

Axel nodded. "I promised you I would. They have to run me through a scanner and look for signs of cancer in six months anyway, so there's no need for you to feel special."

"Then we're going hiking! You said that we could take a trip and we could hike and we could see some truly great things."

"Yes," Axel nodded. "Anywhere you want to go. There's lots of cool places – just pick one, and let me know." After a moment, Axel added a stipulation. "But I want you to promise me something."

"Alright," Partho shrugged.

"Invite your father to go with you first. If he accepts your invitation, you take the trip with him instead."

"Why would I do that?" Partho grimaced. "My father's a prick who'd rather get fat in his chair and smoke cigars and fuck his secretary."

"This has nothing to do with his strength of character – it's about yours. Years from now, I'm pretty sure he will wish to have come with you. And when you look back, you will have been a good son – the kind who invited his father to come along when it was important."

Partho shrugged. "Alright, I'll ask him. But we both know he won't go."

"I know he won't," Axel smiled. "I am so fucking lucky that way."

Axel had never definitively been a father or a son or a grandson or a brother, assuming that momentary and purely technical relationships were not to be included in his calculations. But he had done a pretty good job of surrounding himself with people who provided a wealth of parallel experiences, and then some. All in all, he was pretty damn lucky – when he needed someone to step up, inevitably someone stepped up.

Axel was perfectly willing – eager, in fact – to grab onto the relationships that came his way even if they came secondhand, passed down from perfectly decent people who, for whatever reason, didn't want or didn't have any need of them. Such friendships nearly always turned out the best because they were homemade – and homemade friendship makes a home.

"Tell me something, Axel," Partho said, interrupting Axel's cerebral safari. "Are you going away because your inner-wood nymph told you to?"

"No," Axel laughed, somewhat sheepishly. "I wish I were that sure of myself." Then he thought about it a moment. "But I guess I do feel some responsibility to the others."

"The *others?*" Partho asked, silently praying that this wouldn't involve anything new.

"You know – Odette and Takumi and Axel the first – even 'Frozen Baby Doe.' In fact, I think 'Frozen Baby Doe' could really have been something if she'd had a chance. She would have had a cool English accent and maybe been a little sexy. I want to experience the world for all of them, too."

"They're all *you*, Axel," Partho reminded him. "And I'm not going to stay here if we're just going to fantasize about what a hot English girl you might have become."

Axel took that as his cue to pull himself to his feet and shoulder his backpack. If he sat with Partho a minute longer or spoke another word, he might never leave. He hugged Partho, which didn't feel nearly as silly as either of them expected it would, and in fact carried on longer than any other hug anybody else got that day.

Partho watched Axel hike up over the ridge and called after him. "I'll see you in the spring, asshole!"

"Yes," Axel said, turning back only briefly, and Partho couldn't tell whether he was crying or not. "Have a great senior year, Partho . . . Make good choices!"

"Fuck you, Axel Hooley!" Partho called up toward him, but all he saw was Axel's middle finger as it vanished over the ridge.

Axel continued toward whatever lie ahead – away from Los Angeles and away from his friends, suddenly feeling very small and lonely – which of course was part of his objective in going. He felt plugged in to whatever force had created him and remained convinced that together they would forge mostly auspicious and most assuredly interesting circumstances.

And Axel trusted that the world would be tolerant of his shortcomings because, after all, he was still really new.

*The End*

# Epilogue

Annie welcomed the traveler in the same manner she welcomed all outsiders – warmly, while staying appropriately aloof and at a respectable distance. She certainly needed some work done around the place, what with the boys grown and busy with their own wives and children and farming, and Isaac gone home to his reward lo these past three years or very nearly. And besides, she liked the traveler's face – if she were to have described him (which she didn't), she would have said that the man looked *Biblical* – with his long, flowing, snow-white hair, with but a single streak, black as pitch, shot down the side. And tall – she forever thereafter imagined that he was exactly what one of the Apostles might have looked like (probably Thaddaeus or Bartholemew, she thought – one of the lesser Apostles nobody knows very much about). He gave his name only as Balanos, though she didn't know for certain if it was intended as "Mister Balanos," or "Balanos-with-something-coming-after."

He agreed to stay a couple of weeks, do the work, and sleep in the barn, though they would take the meals Annie cooked together at the same table. She told him all about her six sons and their families, never mentioning the seventh child lost or the curious boy who came after. Such troubling memories were, of course, better off tucked away.

They had such lively exchanges that Annie took to her bed in the evening exhausted and with her head spinning, more often than not with a headache. His ideas about the world and people and creation were all so strange, yet he was interested in what Annie thought and believed, and what she reckoned those beliefs might mean for other folks who didn't live quite so simply or perhaps believed in gods very different from her own.

He even suggested that the two of them were merely traveling different paths, treading around the very same hill, though Annie thought such an idea was just plain silly – Annie and Balanos had never traveled anywhere *near* the same hill as far as she was concerned, particularly with regard to their faith in the Lord.

Balanos said that he didn't believe in a kindly-looking vengeful bearded man who lived up in the clouds, condemning sinners to hellfire and damnation. Whether that is exactly who God is or is not, Annie considered such talk blasphemous. Balanos suggested that God lives within all of us, which was just flowery prideful speech as far as Annie could tell.

It occurred to her later that Balanos might actually have been Satan walking the earth, come round to tempt and confuse her – that, and to patch the side of the barn and muck out the chicken coop.

Balanos finished up his work and left very early on the 10th morning without waking Annie and not having asked her for any money. It was probably all for the best, and maybe even part of Almighty God's great plan.

Annie often thought about the talks they shared together, but two full weeks in his company would have been far too long for both of them.

# Acknowledgments

My cancer diagnosis exploded on Friday the 13th – the cancer was treatable, but the superstitious nature that came along as a chaperone, wasn't. My family was predictably supportive, but timing and fate are twin bitches – my father and brother-in-law were, at the time, enduring the final months of their own ultimately unwinnable cancer battles, and I was reluctant to usurp their caregivers to look after me some 2,000 miles away. Besides, I was athletic, in excellent shape, and had been diagnosed early – I didn't expect it to be a cakewalk, certainly, but undergoing treatment on my own looked to be completely do-able. And so it was . . . for nearly four full days, when my first round of chemotherapy landed me in the hospital and all but slaughtered me.

My own hastily assembled Death Watch List consisted of D.J. Richardson, Laura Buchanan, Michael Annetta, Kay Kudukis, Kaadi Taylor, Ken Metz, Dawn Greenidge, John Money, Jon Larson, Lorna Duyn, Randall Rapstine, Bob Kent, Susan Foster, Josette DiCarlo, Matt McDonald, Tamara Zook, Connie Ventress, Lynn Roof Bercutt, and Vicky Jo Varner. These are my heroes, without whom I would currently inhabit either an urn or a landfill. If they were acting out of anything other than love and compassion, they're screwed because cancer survivors can't be organ donors and nutty cancer fiction doesn't make first-time novelists rich.

Major thanks also go out to far-flung friends who prepared to swoop in to help if needed, including Patricia Motto, Lorinda Grogg, Stacy Embry, LeeAnn Barnard, Jeff & Jackie Evans, Caryl Butterley, Zoë Asprey, Andy Richards, Leta Lenik, Karl Jonason, and the Ammon family. They were such great understudies that they ultimately became part of the cast no matter how many miles stood between us. These are, of course, in addition to my lovely mother, Derexa, and my amazing sister, Tracy, who kept attempting to drive to the airport in defiance of the impossible situation they found themselves in.

Thanks also to Jennifer Cappelletty, Ronn Davids, Shanda Dahl, Michael Tuchin, and all the attorneys and staff at Klee, Tuchin, Bogdanoff & Stern LLP for their determination that I leap whatever hurdles necessary to get well. Special thanks to Kenneth Klee, for his patience, gentle nature, and for taking the time to have the discussions that ultimately led me to channel my anger, fear, and questions into Axel, even though such conversation was incomprehensible to me at the time.

My past is littered with brilliant friends and mentors, all of whom I carry with me, or who managed to weave their way into these pages. Among the notable are Dr. Gilbert Bloom, Gari Williams, Dr. Judy Yordon, Warner Crocker, Marjorie Duehmig-Newson, Maria Elena Rodriguez, and Heather Liston.

Additionally, I would be able to write little more than my name without the tutelage of Russ Tutterow and the fine writers at Chicago Dramatists, and T. Jay O'Brien and the motley batch of lunatics at the Coronet Writers' Lab. Specific gratitude goes to the L.A. Writers Group who braved my first draft: Nicole Criona, Glenn Schwartz, Lisa Kilbride, and Mary Yarber. In addition, I remain indebted to Gary Goldstein, David A. Lee, Daniel Vaillancourt, and the rest of the stouthearted members of WGAw's Gay & Lesbian Writers Committee, as well as WGA staff liaisons Tery Lopez and Kimberly Myers.

Axel Hooley would certainly never have seen the light of day without the encouragement of my supportive early readers – Lisa Delzompo, who pestered me constantly for new chapters, my brother Mark, for advice on magic realism and fantasy fiction,

Lou Evan Caraway, for repeatedly questioning my sanity, Linnea Warren, for editorial advice, and Audrey Newmont, Julie Goldberg, and the wonderfully zany members of their book club, for reading it and for their enthusiastic support.

Thanks also to Bill Kent for the beautiful cover design and Rhonda Tinch-Mize for her superb editing.

It takes an astonishing number of medical personnel to pull a cancer patient through treatment. Thanks to my amazing team: Dr. Daniel Bowers, Dr. David Hoffman, Dr. Leslie Botnick, Dr. Eiman Firoozmand, and the nurses and staff of Tower Hematology & Oncology in Beverly Hills and the Center for Radiation Therapy, Beverly Hills. Thanks also to Dr. Charles Skiba, DO and Ken Howard, LCSW for cobbling me back together in the dark days that inevitably follow such difficult battles.

And lastly, thank you to the wonderful and compassionate citizens of my three beautiful cities – West Hollywood, Beverly Hills, and Los Angeles, who handled me so gently during those fragile and critical life-affirming months. Individually you may consist of more plastic, silicone and space-age polymers than a Honda, but collectively your hearts are solid gold.

–Scotty-Miguel Sandoe
September, 2012

## About the Author

Scotty-Miguel Sandoe is a screenwriter living in West Hollywood, California, where he enjoys the company of better friends than anybody probably deserves. He is an overzealous fan of long bicycle rides, challenging hikes, unskillful surfing, and waking up on days when he doesn't necessarily have cancer.